Dean M. King is an American author who lives with his wife, Kelly, and their son on Northeast Wisconsin's Door Peninsula. He is a member of the Horror Writers Association and the Great Lakes Association of Horror Writers.

Dean finds inspiration for his stories in remote areas of Wisconsin's vast Northwoods, on the islands that lay off its coasts, and among the stalwart bluffs of Southwest Wisconsin. Whether Dean is writing about a dreadful creature that crawled from the Mississippi River or a drag race between a street-toughened hoodlum and the devil, you can be sure—maybe even a little afraid—that his stories will haunt you long after you read the final page.

Dean has published several short stories in online and print venues. *Sarah's Cross* is his first novel.

This is for my beautiful wife, Kelly, who so often said to me, "You should go and write."

Dean M. King

SARAH'S CROSS

A Ghost Story

AUSTIN MACAULEY PUBLISHERS™

LONDON • CAMBRIDGE • NEW YORK • SHARJAH

Ordering Information:
Quantity sales: special discounts are available on quantity purchases by corporations, associations, and others. For details, contact the publisher at the address below.

Publisher's Cataloging-in-Publication data
King, Dean M.
Sarah's Cross: A Ghost Story

ISBN 9781645363415 (Paperback)
ISBN 9781645363408 (Hardback)
ISBN 9781645368922 (Epub e-book)

Library of Congress Control Number: 2019915830

www.austinmacauley.com/us

First Published (2020)
Austin Macauley Publishers LLC
40 Wall Street, 28th Floor
New York, NY 10005
USA

mail-usa@austinmacauley.com
+1 (646) 5125767

I want to thank Michael R. Ritt, a great writer of western fiction and a lifelong friend, whose unceasing encouragement made all the difference in the world.

I also want to thank my mother, JoAnn, for a lifetime of love and encouragement. If there is anything within me that is truly good, I learned it by your example, Mom.

And finally, I would like to thank my readers. I hope I have delivered within these pages a world you easily slip into and characters you won't quickly forget.

Chapter 1
May 5, 1961

I couldn't stop thinking about the little girl. I found her sitting alone by the side of the highway, and the experience of meeting her had been so extraordinary that I scarcely remembered the drive home and turning into my driveway. I didn't see the fawn before it was too late, and the impact sent it sprawling into the gravel.

I climbed out of my old Ford pickup and walked over to the little deer. It lay on its left side with its one visible, unfocused eye shimmering in the glare of my headlights like moonlight reflected on a nighttime lake. Its pink tongue protruded from its velvety muzzle and it panted, even as it shivered. It appeared to be in shock and made no effort to get up. That was good. If any bones were broken, a panicky attempt to stand and flee would be horribly painful.

I crouched down and ran my hands over its silky fur, feeling for broken bones. I found nothing until I examined its front left leg which was curled under its body. There was a long gash on the lower leg, and I thought I glimpsed exposed bone. There was a great deal of blood oozing from the wound, so I pulled my handkerchief from my back pocket and wrapped it tightly around the leg. I worked fast, wanting to finish before the shock wore off and the fawn began panicking. I didn't know how badly it was hurt, and I didn't want it limping off into the woods. A wounded fawn doesn't stand much of a chance against coyotes and hungry bears in the forests of Northeast Wisconsin. I had to keep it safe until I could figure out what to do with it.

I scooped up the fawn and walked toward my garage, a sick feeling working its way into my stomach. Fawns are generally born in April. That meant this one couldn't be more than five or six weeks old. It would still be nursing. I was sure that its mother was somewhere out there in the woods, feeling anxious about her baby, and I feared she would move on soon if I could not return it to her. That couldn't happen until I knew the extent of its injuries.

I left the double swing doors on the front of my garage closed and used the side service door facing the woods. The side door is split in two, so you can open the top half and keep the bottom closed. I pushed it open with my foot and then kicked the lower half closed. I decided to leave the top half open, hopeful that the doe would detect the fawn's scent and remain in the area until I had a better idea of what its future would be.

I pulled the string, and the bare bulb hanging from the rafter glowed into life. I keep an old quilt handy for when I need to crawl under my truck to patch the holes in my muffler with a fresh layer of duct tape. I found it and kicked it into a corner. I made the fawn as comfortable as I could then turned off the light, went back to my truck, and pulled it up to the garage.

I went inside to call Doctor Rayburn. He's the vet who tends most of the cattle and horses in this county and the next over. He answered on the first ring, and I explained what happened. He said he'd be by directly. There was nothing more I could do for now, so I opened a can of RC and sat at my kitchen window where I could look out at the garage and watch for the doe to come searching for her fawn.

I turned on the Philco radio I keep on my small kitchen table, and strangely enough, Bobby Vee was singing "Take Good Care of My Baby." The song was interrupted by President Kennedy, who spent the next several minutes extolling the grand achievement made by Alan Shepard who today had become the first American to travel through space after soaring one hundred and fifteen miles above the earth in a spacecraft named *Freedom 7*. During his speech, the president announced his plan to ask Congress for five hundred and thirty-one million dollars to put a man on the moon.

I thought about that for a moment. The President of the United States wants to spend a half-billion dollars to put a man on the moon, and here I am worrying about a fawn nobody would miss if I had killed it outright. I've always believed that little things matter, and though, while not very important in the grand scheme of things, right now the only help that fawn was going to get was me, and it mattered.

Sure enough, after no more than fifteen minutes of waiting, I saw the doe. I could just barely make out her form emerging from the forest. She moved like an apparition, inching cautiously toward the half-open door of my garage and the scent of her injured baby. She had nearly made it all the way across the open space between the tree line and the garage when she was startled back into the woods by the headlights of Doctor Rayburn's truck. I took my spring jacket from the hook beside the door and stepped outside.

Doctor Rayburn was rummaging around in the bed of his pickup as I approached.

"Hello, sir," I said. "I'm sorry to have called you so late." He turned at the sound of my voice, and I was surprised to see him holding a black case exactly like the bags carried by medical doctors. I don't know why that surprised me, but it did.

"Hello, Tommy," he said. "Had a little mishap with a fawn, huh?"

"Yes, sir. I guess I was a little preoccupied when I pulled in, and I didn't see it until it was too late. I knocked it a good one."

"Well," he said, "let's take a look."

"I have it bedded down in the garage," I said and led the way.

If I have learned anything in my twenty-three years of living, it is that in a polite society, we are to respect others and treat them with dignity. My mother was fond of quoting Thomas Carlyle, and by the age of five, I could recite verbatim, "Every man is my superior in that I may learn from him." My mother believed in showing all people respect through polite conversation. As a result, I tend to speak somewhat formally, especially when in the presence of educated men like physicians. Doctor Rayburn is a man who selflessly committed his life to the healing arts, albeit of animals rather than human beings, and is a hero in my eyes. I hold him in high regard and value the friendship he has shown me these past seven years since treating my now deceased Golden Retriever, Willow, who eventually lost her fight with cancer.

"Sir," I said as we made our way toward my garage, "I hope I didn't take you away from your supper."

"Actually," Doctor Rayburn said, "you saved me from it. Ruth's been experimenting with her cooking again. She reads all those ladies' magazines, you know, *Ladies' Home Journal, Woman's Home Companion, Good Housekeeping*; she gets them all. She experiments with the recipes she finds in them. Tonight, it's something with a French name I can't pronounce, but I'm sure whatever it is she has on the stove, the main ingredient is snails." He smiled broadly and clapped me on the shoulder. "When I'm finished here, I think I'll play it safe and head into town for the meatloaf platter at the diner."

"Yes, sir," I said, smiling.

We reached the garage, and I opened the lower half of the door. "It's back there in the corner," I said, pointing, and pulled on the light. My eyes went immediately to the blood on the floor. It was everywhere, in long streaks and splotches. The corner where I had left the fawn was empty, except for the bloody quilt. "I guess some of the shock has worn off. It was lying quietly when I left it here."

We began searching the garage, looking behind stacks of yellowed newspapers I planned to burn but hadn't gotten to yet and old oil drums I saved to use as burning barrels. I keep an old Ford tractor in the garage. It has a blade for plowing snow from my driveway. I bent low and looked beneath it. The fawn wasn't there. I turned to find Doctor Rayburn and said, "Maybe it managed to jump the half-door."

The rear wall was stacked with boxes containing the things I didn't have room for in my small cabin. Doctor Rayburn was looking into the space behind the stack. "No," he called to me. "Here it is." I walked over and took a look. The fawn had worked itself behind the boxes and appeared to be stuck. There was a lot of blood. We began moving boxes to get at the fawn. It made little effort to get away, and we caught it quickly.

Doctor Rayburn carried the fawn out into the center of the garage where he could examine it under the bare bulb hanging from the rafter. I dragged the quilt out of the corner and spread it on the floor under the light. Doctor Rayburn laid the fawn down, and I restrained it, but it didn't put up much of a struggle.

"It's a little buck," he said, and just as I had done earlier, he began running his hands over the animal, feeling for broken bones. Finding none, he moved on to the injured leg. "Now let's take a look at that leg. Tommy, slide my bag over here." I did, and he took out a large bottle of hydrogen peroxide and sluiced the wound several times, washing away the blood, which had begun to coagulate around the gash.

"It looks bad, sir," I said.

"Actually," he said, "it's not as bad as it looks. At worst, I suspect a hairline fracture."

"Still," I said, gesturing to the floor, "there's all this blood."

"Here," Doctor Rayburn said to me, "hold his leg like this." He showed me how and then began taking various items from his bag. As he worked, he said, "There's not much flesh on the foreleg of a deer. It's just hide-covered bone. Nature has designed deer to withstand the cold winters we have here in Wisconsin. For example, the hairs in their coat are hollow and air-filled. It's excellent insulation. All that fur is nourished with blood from a vast network of capillaries. There are even more capillaries in the extremities where there is little fat or flesh and a greater need for blood to warm the appendage. The wound to that leg looks worse than it is because of all those capillaries in the skin. It's like a minor scalp wound in a human. Have you ever had one?" he asked.

"Yes, sir," I said. "I've had a few."

"I'll bet they bled like a son of a gun, didn't they?"

"Well," I said, "now that you mention it, I do recall scaring the bejesus out of my mother the time I fell off the monkey bars at a park when I was a boy. I hit my head on a jagged piece of concrete, and by the time I walked home, I had blood all over my face and soaked into the collar of my white tee shirt. My mother nearly fainted when I came through the door, but she got me cleaned up, and it turned out to be just a fair-sized cut to my scalp."

Nodding, Doctor Rayburn said, "The wound in that leg is very much like your scalp wound. All the blood makes it look worse than it is." He squatted down, "Still, I can't be absolutely sure without doing an x-ray, but it's a pretty safe bet there's at least a slight fracture. It's going to be tough for this little guy to survive out there long enough for that leg to heal, even with the doe looking after him. By the way, have you seen the doe?"

"I saw her making her way toward the garage just as you turned into my driveway. Your lights spooked her," I said. "I guess that she's still out there somewhere close by."

Doctor Rayburn shook his head solemnly and said, "My recommendation is that I put him out of his misery. Compared with what he's facing out there with that bad leg, it's the humane thing to do."

I thought about this for a moment then said, "What if I were to care for him, you know, feed him and tend to the leg until he's healed sufficiently to be released? The leg will heal, won't it?"

"Oh, it will heal over time," Doctor Rayburn said, "but it could take a few months to heal completely, and without the doe to teach him to get along in the wild, he's likely to fall prey to a wolf or a pack of coyotes within days of release."

I thought some more, then asked, "Could you rig up a temporary bandage or cast, something that will break away in time? I could keep him until he's got his strength back. I can keep the upper door open so the doe will scent him. Maybe she'll stay near. Maybe in a few days he'll be stronger, and I can get them back together."

"A few days are all I recommend," Doctor Rayburn said. "I give it about 72 hours before the doe gives up on him and moves on. What about feeding him?" he asked.

I thought about it for a moment and said, "Don't farmers use bottles to feed calves they separate from their mothers?"

Doctor Rayburn was nodding. "They do," he said. "And they feed them a milk replacer. It's got all the nutrition they need since they're cut off from their mother's milk." He was silent for a moment. "It might work," he said. "It might work."

We spent the next half hour rigging a break-away cast that Doctor Rayburn pronounced capable of supporting the leg but fragile enough to fall away over time. "It's a lot of bother for one little fawn," he said, while wrapping layers of plaster-soaked gauze around the wound, but he seemed pleased with his work. "The woods are full of deer. They're all over the roads around here. You're not the first one to hit a deer, you know. Why are you doing this?"

I thought for a moment, considering whether or not to tell him about the little girl and how it had caused me to start thinking about just how precious and fragile life is, regardless of whether that life belongs to a human or a fawn. I could have told him everything, but I decided against it. Not only because he was unlikely to believe a word of my story—he would, in fact, very likely peg me as some sort of loony—but because I had a lot to do before I would understand everything that had happened to me on my drive home this evening and what I was going to do about it.

"I know it is," I said, "but I'd like to try. I live alone here and I have the time. If I can get him to eat and keep him from making that wound worse, maybe he'll be ready to go back to his mother in a few days. If not, there's always the other option."

Doctor Rayburn smiled as he finished the tiny cast. "I'll stop by early tomorrow with a bottle and some milk replacer. He'll be good and hungry by then. If you can get him to eat, I'd say he stands a pretty good chance of surviving. If not…" he trailed off. "Well, let's just see how it goes, shall we?" He smoothed the last layer of plaster and gauze and said, "There, that should do the trick."

I carried the fawn back to the corner after replacing the quilt. He made no attempt to get up and seemed to be on the verge of sleep. We left the garage, leaving the top half of the door open, and went to my cabin so Doctor Rayburn could wash up. "Can I get you a cup of coffee?" I asked.

"No, thank you, Tommy. I guess I had better get home and try my wife's snail stew," he said, grimacing.

"What do I owe you, sir?" I asked.

"No charge," he said. "That's a wild animal out there in your garage. I don't charge for service rendered to strays or wild animals."

"That's very generous of you, sir," I said. "Thank you." I walked Doctor Rayburn to his truck, thanked him again, and watched him back out of my driveway and head for home.

I have been renting this cabin since graduating from high school six years ago when I was seventeen. The cottage and forty acres of woods belong to Ted Morgan, a man who lives in Milwaukee and who had been a friend of my father up until the time of my father's death when I was just ten years old. He and my father hunted deer together since before I was born, but my father's passing brought an abrupt end to their hunting, and the old cabin went unused after that. By the time I was old enough to drive, the cabin had fallen into disrepair. Ted's health had also declined, and he could no longer make the four-hour trip north from Milwaukee, so he hired me to look after the place.

Once a week for two years, I made the twelve-mile round trip drive from my home in Joshua Falls to maintain the lawn and keep the cabin weather-tight. After graduating high school, Ted and I made an agreement that I could rent it for a very reasonable rate as long as I continued to keep it up, which I am happy to do. The firewood I take off the forty acres keeps the cabin warm in the winter, and the sugaring I do in the spring produces enough maple syrup to sell to summer tourists and supplements the wages I make working full-time at the quarry in a little town named Alibi, which sits just south of the Michigan border.

I do not have a girlfriend, though I am not opposed to a romantic entanglement. Someday, when the right girl comes along, I'll be blessed to have her share my life, but for now, I enjoy the solitude of living alone. I purposefully live a frugal life, unfettered by debt and the pursuit of possessions.

I am most certainly not the typical twenty-three-year-old, in that I find my riches in the beauty of my surroundings and a contemplative life focused on higher things than the latest fads in fashion or music. My work at the quarry is satisfying enough, and I have all I need in the warm glow of my fireplace and the cold glow of my refrigerator when I open the door and peer inside.

I watched Doctor Rayburn's taillights until he rounded the bend in the road, and then I turned my eyes to the night sky. Living as far from town as I do, there is no light pollution to dim the radiance of God's celestial masterpiece. My sky is a vast, black tapestry shot through with a million pinpricks of light, and on moonless nights, the Orion Nebula feels close enough to touch.

As I stood there marveling over the enormity and complexity of the cosmos, as I always do when I am outside at night, I wondered what it would be like to look down on this planet from one hundred and fifteen miles up in space, completely isolated and alone. Would I feel euphoric and exhilarated or profound loneliness in the face of complete separation from all of humanity?

Though I choose to live alone, my spirit is strengthened by the knowledge that there are those who care for me. I have acquaintances at work, friends with whom I correspond, and family to visit during the holidays. I love and know that am loved in return. When I am standing alone under a seemingly horizonless nighttime sky, I am not truly separated from those who care for me, for I am free to come and go and place myself within their loving reach.

Gazing up at the enormity of the heavens, I thought of Alan Shepherd having made his journey alone in his spacecraft more than one hundred miles above the surface of the earth, and I wondered what would have happened if something had gone terribly wrong and he had been unable to return to earth some fifteen minutes after launch? What would it be like to be completely separated from everyone who cares for me, cut off from all contact with no hope of ever being in the presence of those who make glad my needy heart?

Just then, a shooting star with an impossibly bright tail streaked across the sky and disappeared beyond the tall firs to the east. As I watched its trail glow in the night sky and then fade away, I found myself once again thinking about the little girl.

Chapter 2

Eagle Bluff is a steep grade that marks the halfway point along my twenty-mile commute on State Road 141 between my cabin and the stone quarry at Alibi, a small town on the border of Wisconsin and the Upper Peninsula of Michigan. The ride home takes me through a vast area of unbroken forest comprised of tens of thousands of acres of spruce, fir, maple, and birch and scattered tamarack wetlands. Only occasionally does one encounter a residence, and they are usually well secluded at the end of long driveways. These tiny outposts are nearly all seasonal cabins built by hunters and fisherman who visit them infrequently throughout the year. There is very little traffic along this stretch of highway, and I have found it prudent to keep extra gasoline and a chainsaw in the box of my pickup. I never know when I will need to remove a fallen tree from the road.

It was about 7:30 in the evening with the sun hanging just above the horizon in a deepening violet sky. I spotted the little girl as soon as my truck topped Eagle Bluff. Her yellow dress stood out brightly against the emerald green of the spring foliage. She was sitting on a birch log near an immense pine tree where the ditch grass met the forest. A big grin broke out on her face when she saw me, and she jumped to her feet and began bouncing up and down, frantically waving at me. Shocked to see a little girl all alone so far from the nearest house, I pulled over in the grass and got out.

She appeared to be only eight or nine years old and delicately built. She was fair-skinned with a round face and full lips. Her eyes were the palest shade of blue, and though she appeared happy that I had stopped, they managed to retain a melancholy expression. Her yellow summer dress had a wide lace collar that covered her narrow shoulders like a cape. Her white sun hat had a generous brim and rested on the back of her head, allowing her beautiful, blonde hair the opportunity to glimmer in the last light of the day.

"Hello there," I said. "I'm Tommy Ryan. Who are you?" She looked up at me with an anxious expression. Her eyes darted back and forth as she looked me over, reminding me of the finches that flit between the trees and the bird feeder hanging by my kitchen window. She finished sizing me up by looking intently into my eyes, and it had the effect of making me feel as if she were looking deep inside of me rather than at me.

She reached out and took my hand in hers. Her white cotton gloves felt cool and smooth, her touch, feather light. Using only her eyes, she directed my gaze toward the enormous pine tree standing at the edge of the woods where she had been sitting when I first spotted her. We remained that way for a moment, hand in hand, looking at the tree, and then she started forward, tugging me along, forcing me to go with her.

We stopped a few feet from the pine, and I glanced up to take in its height and was surprised to see dozens of glossy, black crows resting in its branches. What astonished me was not that they were there—the Northwoods is full of crows and ravens—but that they were utterly silent and not their usual raucous self. I looked back at the little girl, and she released my hand and pointed at the base of the enormous tree.

I looked where she was indicating but could see nothing. Her anxious expression intensified, and she jabbed her finger at the tree, silently conveying her insistence. I stepped up to the tree and bent to take a close look. I pulled back some brush that was covering its base and saw a large area of bark was missing. It appeared to be an old scar about the size of a supper plate. The wood where the bark was absent was weathered gray and smooth. The edge of the bark surrounding the missing patch was well healed over.

"Is this what you want me to see?" I asked, looking back at her. She nodded. "Won't you speak to me?" I asked. She ignored my question and gestured for me to come close to her. I did, and she again took my hand. I squatted in front of her; I asked again if she would speak. She said nothing. Instead, she pointed at the ground and made sweeping motions with her hand, as if calling my attention to the thick mat of dead grass that until only recently had been covered by several inches of snow.

"Have you lost something?" I asked scanning the ground. "Is that why you're out here? Do you want me to help you find it?"

She nodded enthusiastically, and I began parting the brown tufts with my boot looking for whatever was causing

23

her to behave so impatiently. I wandered about kicking through the thick, matted grass for a while until I felt my boot hit something. I reached into the grass and felt a stiff, slender object pressed against the cold earth. It was tangled deeply in layers of seasons-old grass, and it took a moment for me to pull it free. When I did, I held it up in the dying light and examined it.

It was a little cross made from two thin wooden slats bound where they crossed by several layers of rusting wire. The upright portion was about thirty inches long and appeared to have been snapped off at the base. The cross member was perhaps twelve inches in length. It was coated with whitewash, but the paint was badly oxidized and chalky. Whoever had placed the cross out here had painted SARAH on the cross member and 1948 on the upright slat. I have seen similar crosses in my travels. They are generally placed at the scenes of fatal accidents to honor the memory of those who have died.

I looked at the little girl and saw that her eyes had filled with tears. They shimmered in the day's last light as she looked from my eyes to the cross and back to my eyes again. I had no idea what to make of it. Why was this little girl all alone along such a deserted stretch of highway so far from any house, and what was her interest in the cross? The sight of it deeply moved her. The logical conclusion was that she has some connection to this Sarah who had ostensibly died here in 1948, but the girl remained silent and left me to wonder if Sarah had been a member of her family, perhaps a sister or a favorite aunt?

I was just about to reach down to cup her cheek and ask these questions when she disappeared. I don't mean that she dashed into the woods or ran down the road. She hadn't slipped behind a tree and hid in a thicket. She vanished. One moment she was there, as real and three dimensional as me, and the next she dissolved into nothing. Her image wholly faded before my eyes.

All I could do was stare at the place where she had been standing. A cold finger traced an icy track down my spine, and I felt the hairs on my arms stand on end. I swallowed hard and started for my truck but then saw movement and looked toward the big pine. The little girl was seated on the birch log again, but this time, the liveliness was gone, and her slight frame convulsed as she cried silently into her gloved hands.

I am not a particularly brave person, and I am indeed no kind of authority on things supernatural, but the sight of this silently crying little girl was more heartrending than frightening. I was still holding the cross, and I walked over to her. I must admit that it took me a moment to summon my courage, but eventually, I sat beside her on the log. I asked, "Is this your cross? Did somebody place it here in your memory? Is your name Sarah?"

She looked up at me slowly, and then I perceived only the slightest nod of her head.

Tears began streaming from her eyes as if merely hearing her name spoken aloud had opened the floodgates of her emotions, yet through her tears, the prettiest smile I had ever seen graced her face. Any trepidation I was feeling about coming face to face with a ghost left me completely at the sight of that innocent smile. I asked her, "Why are you here, Sarah? Can't you move on?" She answered my questions by shaking her head.

I am the first to admit that I have limited knowledge of the afterlife, but everything I had ever heard about the topic suggested that the departed were supposed to enter some other plane of existence. Whether this is heaven or merely another life on some level that those in this life cannot perceive, I have no firm opinion, but for some reason, Sarah lingered in the place where her young life had ended some thirteen years earlier, and she was either unable or unwilling to tell me why.

I took both of her hands in mine and did my best to comfort her, but how does one comfort the dead? What words could mitigate the pain she felt and the loneliness she had endured these past thirteen years, tethered to this lonely stretch of country highway while the world moved on? I felt her grip on my hands tighten, and I marveled at the astonishing fact that I was holding hands with a ghost.

Sarah released one of my hands and with her free hand, directed my attention once more to the big pine tree. As the last rays of sunlight illuminated the uppermost branches of the ancient pine, I suddenly understood what she was telling me. Thirteen years ago, perhaps in the spring of 1948, the car in which Sarah was a passenger left the road and struck the pine tree, killing her. Sometime afterward, someone had crafted the cross to honor her memory and pushed it into the ground at the site where she died. Eventually, time and the elements had succeeded in blotting out the memory of that fateful day. The cross was broken off, most likely by a passing snowplow, and became mired under layers of decaying grass until I pulled it free.

I remained seated next to Sarah for a long while, looking into her innocent face, touched by her sweetness and sorrow, and when I felt a drop of moisture strike my hand, only then did I realized that I, too, was crying. Seeing my pain, she pulled me down to her level, and slipping her thin arms around my neck, Sarah embraced me. Her touch was warm and real, and I detected a faint aroma of lilac.

We stayed that way for several minutes, and as darkness lifted out of the forest consigning daylight to the tips of the tallest fir trees at the top of Eagle Bluff, Sarah sobbed silently against my neck. After a time, I felt her grip loosen, and she sat up straight and seemed to compose herself.

Something drew my attention again to the crows sitting in the pine high above me. I got to my feet and looked up. There were many more birds than when I first noticed them. Somehow, they had arrived without making a sound, and they now lined every branch that was thick enough to support their collective weight. Clustered wing to wing, the ugly horde stared down with their tiny, black bead eyes boring straight into me.

She belongs to the Empty!

The thought came from nowhere. It pushed its way into my mind like a schoolyard bully cuts into line. I had no idea what it meant, but for a flicker of a moment, I felt utterly lost and alone and…empty. It was a dreadful feeling, dark and despairing, and it hit me just as the entire flock of crows lifted off in unison and began a frantic flight back and forth just above my head. Several of the birds dipped dangerously low, and I had to duck and cover my head with my arms to avoid their beaks. The crazed birds were no longer silent. They screamed their raspy caw furiously as they soared back and forth in swooping arcs that came within inches of striking me.

I snatched a glance at Sarah and saw a look of abject fear in her eyes. She began pulling on my arm, urging me toward the forest. I went with her, and shortly after entering the woods, the angry screams of the crows faded. I thought we would wait just inside the trees until we were sure they had gone, but Sarah dropped my hand and headed deeper into the woods. She took several steps and then turned and, rather insistently, beckoned me to follow her.

I followed, but without a flashlight, I was feeling anxious about being in the forest after dark. It was difficult going for me. Branches and fallen logs impeded my progress, and it took an effort to thread my way through, but Sarah moved through the dense woods with ease, seemingly without disturbing a single leaf or snapping a twig under her foot.

We walked on that way for several minutes until we stepped into a small clearing at the edge of a large lake which I did not recognize. That didn't surprise me in the least. With more than fifteen thousand named and unnamed freshwater lakes scattered across the state, many entirely contained within the boundaries of large tracts of privately held land, it is entirely possible to go a lifetime without knowing of the existence of a lake such as the one I was seeing. If there is no public access, no road sign pointing the way to a boat launch or beach, the lake could remain forever hidden and unknown to all but the landowner and pilots flying high above the seemingly endless Northern Wisconsin forest.

The sun had fully set, causing the eastern sky to take on a deep violet as the earth's shadow projected itself above the horizon. Not even the slightest breeze rippled the water nor disturbed the evening mist drifting above the lake's glassy surface. As we stood at the edge of the lake, spring peepers and croaking bullfrogs treated us to an unmelodious chorus, and above it all, the mournful cry of a loon sent a shiver down my spine.

Leave her. She belongs to the Empty!

The thought entered my mind again. It was as if I were picking it up like a receiver picks up a radio signal. I didn't know what it meant, but a profound feeling of desolation accompanied it, and I hoped I would never feel misery like that again.

Could this misery belong to Sarah?

As I stood there with Sarah taking in the splendor of the lake at dusk, I wondered if she was able to appreciate the beauty of the scene as I did. Do spirits see loveliness in sunsets as do the living, or does that characteristic of their humanity perish with their physical body? Was it possible that on the day before her young life ended, Sarah had looked upon her last sunset with the ability to be moved in her soul by the pure glory of the event? One hears so many stories of spirits haunting the places where they died, as if tethered there by chains of sorrow, bound to the earth by sadness and grief. I hoped that Sarah was experiencing the beauty of the scene before us as I was at that moment and that whatever emotions earthbound spirits retained, the ability to appreciate the serenity of a sunset lake was among them.

As if in answer to my contemplations, Sarah looked up at me with brimming eyes and took my hand in hers. Then a smile so sweet as to be incongruous with the sorrow in her eyes came to her face, and we turned back to gazing across the lake. After a moment, Sarah tugged on my hand to gain my attention again and pointed across the still water to a large house on the far shore.

I hadn't noticed it before, but an exterior light had come on and the house, though distant, was clearly visible. I stood there trying to get my bearings, but without any idea of how far we had walked through the forest, it was difficult to get a fix on my location. The lake was likely contained within a large tract of private land where I had never had a reason to venture. During the post-war boom years, many wealthy families had acquired large tracts of Northern Wisconsin land with private lakes and built magnificent summer homes after the fashion of the great camps of Vanderbilt and Rockefeller, such as are found in the Adirondacks of Upstate New York. Once acquired, these magnificent private preserves were jealously guarded against public intrusion, and the families often remained out of sight and secretive. Looking around and seeing no other lights, it was apparent the house stood alone on an otherwise undeveloped lake. I could see the light reflecting off windows but could make out no other detail of the house.

"What is it, Sarah? Is that your home?" She nodded, and for the first time since encountering her, hope seemed to reside in her eyes. "Is there something you want me to do for you?" I asked. She nodded again, this time more enthusiastically, and then began a series of hand gestures and facial expressions to communicate what she wanted. I was not getting it. I had no idea at all what she wanted from me.

Darkness was fully upon us now, and as I gazed across the obsidian surface of the lake, I wondered about the light over there and who might be home and what Sarah wanted me to do. After a few moments more of pantomime, Sarah gave up trying to communicate with me, and I resisted the urge to ask her questions. Despite her frustration at my inability to understand her, she again seemed content merely looking across the water, and I did not want to risk distressing her.

I was diverted from my pondering when I felt Sarah release my hand. When I glanced down, she was gone. I turned and investigated the woods, wondering how I would find my way back in near total darkness, and was astonished to see a faint glowing trail leading back the way we had come. A residue of Sarah's radiance rested upon every branch and leaf she had touched along the way. I followed her trail back to the road without stumbling and hurting myself and climbed behind the wheel of my truck. I wondered if I would sleep at all tonight.

Chapter 3

Doctor Rayburn was true to his word and arrived early the next morning with a bottle and a bag of the powdered milk replacer he had said he would drop off. He checked the cast he had put on the fawn's leg the night before and pronounced it "a pretty damn good job of cobbling." I was afraid the fawn wouldn't take anything, but he drank the milk replacer from the bottle just like he was sucking on its momma's teat. I had a full day planned and knew he would get hungry again before I returned home, so I let him drink his fill. I didn't see the doe, but I could hear her back in the woods, stamping her hooves and snorting. I was encouraged that she had remained close to her baby all night.

I invited Doctor Rayburn in for breakfast, but he declined citing a full schedule of farm visits, and I watched him drive off. I went back into my cabin and fried bacon and eggs and brewed strong coffee, and while I ate, I searched my old county map trying to figure out which lake Sarah had led me to the night before. This part of Wisconsin is a vast, relatively unbroken forest dotted with thousands of lakes. Many are unnamed and unmapped. My efforts at finding it on my county map proved fruitless, and I decided that I would have to drive the back roads north of Eagle

Bluff and look for a driveway or a forest road that would take me to the house I had seen last night on the far side of the lake.

It was Friday, and if I were to play hooky from work, I would have the weekend to look into this most unusual mystery. I called the quarry and told my boss that I was not up to coming in. He told me to feel better, and I felt worse for lying to him. I don't like to mislead people, but I didn't know how I could explain what I was up to without having him think me completely mad.

I packed a lunch, checked on the fawn one last time, and then climbed into my pickup. Twenty minutes later, the big birch log where I had seen Sarah sitting the evening before came into view. In the full light of day, I felt somewhat foolish about the episode I had experienced the night before. It was just a big pine, a bunch of crows, and an overactive imagination. They had been startled by something and had not been attacking.

Only they were attacking, Tommy boy. They were, and there was something dark and unnatural in it.

I slowed to look for Sarah, but she was not present, or if she was, she was not visible to me. I found myself saddened by the thought that I may never see her again. Clearly, she had reached out to me for some purpose which I had yet to discover. Surely her communications with me would be ongoing until I had satisfied her unspoken request.

I pulled to the side of the road and looked at the place where Sarah had led me into the forest the evening before. While searching for the exact location, my foot struck something, and I looked down to see the little cross with SARAH and 1948 hand painted on the upright and cross member. I picked it up and thought, *You didn't imagine her.* I leaned the cross against the base of a tall fir and went back to searching for the place where I had followed Sarah into the woods.

I located a spot where the grass and forest ferns were trodden and stepped into the woods to try to get a sense for how far we had walked before coming to the shore of the lake. I estimated that we had gone in a northeasterly direction for approximately twenty minutes. The average person walks at roughly four miles per hour over unobstructed ground. Given that I had walked through dense forest at half that speed, I estimated that I had walked approximately a half-mile before coming to the lakeshore. The house I had seen was roughly three-quarters of a mile away at the northeast end of the lake, putting it approximately a mile and a quarter northeast of the point where I was standing.

I went back to my truck and drove west looking for the first opportunity to turn north onto a side road. It was a mile and a half before I came to the first road to the north. Halls Road was a narrow lane cutting a path through the dense forest like a gravel scar on green skin. I turned down the road and began looking for a driveway or road that would take me to the mystery house. Twenty minutes later, I had tried two narrow lanes that went east, but abruptly ended a short distance into the forest and were most likely access roads for hunters.

I went back to Halls Road and continued north and soon came to a third road heading into the forest in an easterly direction. This unnamed road, like the other two I had ventured down, was narrow and paved with gravel. I turned in and immediately doubted my decision. Low-hanging branches scraped across my windshield and snagged on my side mirrors. Twice I had to get out to clear fallen tree limbs from my path. At last, after driving what seemed to be about one mile, I drove out of the trees and into a large grassy clearing.

The gravel road continued for another hundred yards and then disappeared around the side of a majestic old home that was large enough to be called stately but too small to be referred to as a mansion. I looked to my right and, through a copse of tall fir trees, caught a glimpse of sunlight reflecting off water. It all meshed perfectly with what I had seen last evening. I had found the mystery house Sarah had shown me from across the lake.

I climbed out of my truck and stood by the open door taking in my surroundings. The breeze was coming from the direction of the lake and the morning air was redolent with pine and dew-dampened earth and the aroma of the trout lily that covered the forest beneath the maples, basswood, and hemlocks. A cluster of Jack-in-the-pulpit had thrust up from the soil near a rotting stump to my left, and everywhere, nodding trillium were preparing to bloom. Somehow it seemed less intrusive to leave my truck parked where it was and walk to the house, and as I made my way along the gravel driveway, I took in the view of the magnificent home.

It stood bright and cheery before the glimmering lake. The breeze tumbled waves onto a rocky shore about one hundred yards from the home's expansive front porch where I could see a bench swing creaking back and forth at the ends of its chains. Sunlight reflected off numerous glass panes, and here and there, great billows of lacy curtain drifted out of open windows on the morning breeze before disappearing back inside.

Festooned with gingerbread, spindles and patterned shingles, and painted two shades of gray with burgundy and cream-colored trim, the classic Queen Anne towered three stories and an attic above a thick foundation of quarried granite blocks. The roof was steeply pitched and irregular. Massive classical columns resting on stone piers supported the roof of a sprawling wrap-around porch. At one corner, a turret towered above the house, lending to its asymmetrical appearance. Windows with dentil moldings adorned the turret, conforming to its gracefully curved surface. A cobblestone walkway led away from the front porch to a large, burbling, multi-tiered fountain centered within a circular reflecting pool. Fragrant iris, hyacinth and bright red and yellow tulips bordered the walk and rimmed the pool. From the porch and windows on this side of the house, one would have a commanding view of the lake, which shimmered like a field of diamonds at the end of a vast, well-groomed lawn.

As I stood admiring the grand structure, I heard a woman's voice calling to me. I looked toward the rear of the house, where it was closest to the forest, and saw her emerge from the shadow of a sprawling maple. She began walking toward me, so I remained where I was standing and waited for her to approach.

She was tall and slender and moved with an elegance that made her appear as if she were gliding across the expanse of lawn that lay between us. She carried a basket of cut spring flowers in one gloved hand, and the other held pruning scissors. Her hair was held in place by a scarf which she had tied on top of her head to keep it from falling across her eyes. Though dressed somewhat formally in a high-waisted pleated skirt and a checked blouse rolled up to mid-forearm, the smudge of dirt on her left cheek and the items she carried implied that she was engaged in garden work. As she drew nearer, I recognized her sandals as being quite like the style my mother used to wear when enjoying casual time out of doors. The uppers were made from soft leather while the soles were fashioned from wood, skillfully carved and hinged so the wearer could walk easily and bend her feet naturally. I had not seen this style for many years.

"May I help you?" she said as she removed the gardening gloves from her hands and tucked an errant strand of hair back under the scarf.

She appeared to be in her mid-thirties and was quite lovely. She had the pale, flawless face of one who eschewed the sun as a rule. Her makeup was expertly applied and entirely incongruous with the smudge on her cheek. I had to work hard to prevent myself from laughing. Fortunately, a smile was in order, so I put on my best and greeted her.

"Hello, ma'am," I said, taking off my hat. "My name is Tommy Ryan. I hope you'll forgive the intrusion. Are you the owner of this property?"

She set the basket on the ground and crossed her arms. If she was nervous about finding a strange man standing on her lawn, her expression didn't give it away, but I noticed that she held onto the pruning scissors.

"My name is Vanessa Reissman...Mrs. Robert Reissman. What can I do for you, Mr. Ryan?"

"Well…" I began and then stopped, realizing that I didn't know where to start or what to say. Sarah had led me to the shore of the lake and directed my attention to this house but had either not been willing or was unable to tell me what she wanted me to do. My efforts this morning had been entirely about locating the house. I hadn't planned out what I would do when I found it. What was I going to say to this woman? *Excuse me, ma'am, but the ghost of a little girl led me into the forest on the far side of the lake last night and pointed out your home to me. Uh, could you maybe tell me what it all means?*

I have always believed that honesty is the best policy and didn't want to deceive this lady, but I also believe in using the common sense the Lord gave me, and common sense was telling me to approach this situation at an angle slightly less than head-on. I said, "I'm your neighbor from the other side of Eagle Bluff. I work over in Alibi, and on my way home last evening, I struck and injured a deer."

This was not entirely untrue, as I had hit the fawn in my driveway, but I left the details vague and pressed on. "I found it necessary to walk into the forest north of the state road, and I ended up on the far side of your lake," I said, nodding my head toward the water. "It was right at sunset, and I saw the lights come on in your house. I didn't know there was a house over here on this side of the lake. In fact, I didn't even know there was a lake here."

She was quiet for a beat and then said, "That is because the lake and all of the land surrounding it are private. They have been so for generations. There is no public access, nor are there any roads, apart from the highway, which is within a half-mile of the shoreline. My husband's family has owned this land for many years, Mr. Ryan, and we treasure our privacy. Summer Rest, that is what my husband's family named this place, is our sanctuary. It is our place of refuge when we need to escape the trials of city life. You see," she said, "we are from Chicago. It is a marvelous city, Mr. Ryan, with much to offer by way of culture and sophistication, but it can be an exhausting place, and one grows tired of concrete and steel extending in all directions as well as the attitudes of ignorant people."

"Yes, ma'am," I said.

She had been squinting up at me uncomfortably. "May I offer you some shade, Mr. Ryan?" she asked and gestured toward the large covered porch facing the fountain.

"That would be nice," I said, and followed her toward the house. "If you don't mind my asking, what business is your husband in?"

We arrived at the steps to the porch, and she gestured toward comfortable looking wicker furniture arranged under an expansive window, which, no doubt provided an impressive view of the front lawn and the lake from within the parlor.

"Banking," she said. "My husband's family has been involved in the financial trades for many decades." Mrs. Reissman placed her basket and the pruning shears on a glass-topped coffee table that sat amid the arrangement of furniture and said, "My exertions this morning have given me a thirst. May I offer you a drink, Mr. Ryan?"

I was quite thirsty and replied, "Water would be fine. Thank you."

"Please make yourself comfortable," she said, and disappeared into the house. I took a seat in one of a pair of high-backed wicker chairs facing a loveseat, and she was back shortly with a pitcher of ice water and two glasses. She sat across from me on the loveseat and poured two glasses of water. We were quiet for a moment as I sipped from my glass, but Mrs. Reissman left hers on the coffee table between us and ignored it.

"And what of yourself?" she asked, picking up the thread of conversation as if it had not been interrupted by her trip into the house. "Are your people local to this area?"

"Yes, ma'am," I said. "My father and mother were both born and raised in these parts. It's the only home I have ever known."

She seemed to consider my words for a moment and then said, "You are fortunate to have spent your entire life in such beautiful surroundings. I was born and raised in Chicago, but I am staying here while my husband is serving overseas."

"Your husband is a military man?" I asked.

"Yes. My Robert is a captain in the United States Army," she said with pride, but I couldn't miss something in her eyes that spoke silently of great sadness, which was to be expected with a husband serving away from home.

I had recently read in the news that South Vietnam had signed a military and economic aid treaty with the United States and support troops were being sent to Vietnam under the newly formed Military Assistance Command. I asked, "How long has your husband been in Vietnam?"

She furrowed her brow and cocked her head slightly to one side and said, "My husband is not in Vietnam, Mr. Ryan. He is serving in the war in the Pacific."

I was confused. The war in the Pacific had ended in 1945 in the wake of the bombings of Nagasaki and Hiroshima. I know that the United States maintains a military presence in Europe, but I was less informed about our presence in the Pacific. "Is your husband involved in a diplomatic mission?" I asked.

"The fighting there can hardly be described as diplomacy, Mr. Ryan. Diplomacy generally does not make use of bullets and bombs. No," she said, "my Robert is commander of an entire rifle company. He is responsible for the lives of nearly two hundred men." Her expression became melancholy, and she said, "My Robert is with the Sixth Army fighting at the Lingayen Gulf on Luzon in the Philippines. I have not heard from him since the invasion in January, but I am certain he is alright. It is terribly difficult to get mail out of a war zone."

Her words baffled me. The invasion at Lingayen Gulf had taken place toward the end of World War II, yet Mrs. Reissman was speaking of it as if it had only occurred a few months earlier. She saw the confusion on my face and said, "Surely you are keeping up to date on current events, Mr. Ryan. With all the tragedy and turmoil in the world, you must read the newspapers and listen to Mr. Murrow on the radio."

I have heard of psychic visions. I have read about such things with great interest, and, according to my paternal grandmother, we Ryan's have a history of keen insight bordering on the preternatural, something she always referred to as "the knowing." I have never given the idea of special insight much faith, but the images that ran through my mind as I listened to Vanessa speak of her soldier husband caused me to rethink my grandmother's claims about our theoretical family trait. I saw images in my mind's eye that were as clear and animated as any witnessed with the naked eye. I saw Vanessa Reissman meticulously preserving in place things last touched by her loving husband. I saw her standing at the living room window with the curtain pulled back, gazing across the front lawn, keeping a welcoming light glowing in expectation of an arrival, and I saw her lying alone on one side of a marriage bed, eyes red-rimmed, ears alert for the distant sound of an automobile coming down the driveway. I do not know for certain whether the images I saw so clearly were the product of my imagination or "the knowing," but I could quite clearly feel the weight of the vigil Vanessa Reissman was lovingly maintaining in expectation of a homecoming that was sixteen years overdue. It was as heavy a burden as any human being had been forced to endure while waiting for news of a loved one gone off to war.

I looked at the lady and was struck by the fact that though she seemed physically whole and, for the most part, rational, Vanessa Reissman was living with the belief that America was still fighting the war with Japan and that her husband was bravely commanding his rifle company in the jungles of the Philippines.

"Mr. Ryan? Are you quite all right?"

"Huh?"

"I asked you if you are keeping up on current events."

I am nothing, if not a nimble thinker, and I recovered smoothly. "Of course, I am doing my best to stay current," I said, "but I have no family members serving, and my work keeps me quite busy. That's a poor excuse, I know, but it's accurate."

Mrs. Reissman gave me a disapproving look but didn't press the issue. She had picked up her glass of water but hadn't yet taken a sip. She set it back on the table with the pitcher and smiled at me. I made a show of looking around. "Are you here alone?" I asked. "I don't mean to pry, but Summer Rest is a large estate. You must have some staff to assist you."

She seemed to give it careful thought before answering, but then said, "Oh, yes. They are usually flitting about tending to the house and grounds, but today is their day off, and they tend to make themselves scarce on their day off. I suppose they are afraid I will require something rigorous of them if they are anywhere within my sight. They deserve a day for leisure, but it leaves me quite alone once each week."

She laughed at this statement, and her smile was lovely, but there was something behind her smile that hinted at information she didn't want me to have. It seemed odd to me that this refined lady, born and raised in a big city, would feel comfortable in such a remote setting. I had yet to find a way to bring up Sarah and my reason for being here, and this seemed like the opening I was waiting for.

"Is there no other family here with you in this big house?" I asked casually. "Are you staying here with your husband's family? Do you have children?" Her smile faded quickly, and she was silent for a long moment, and in her eyes, I detected the slightest glint of fear. I couldn't help but feel as if I had added to her grief by asking about family. For just a moment, I saw the muscles in her jaw flex as if she were biting down hard on something bitter, and when she responded, it was only with a curt, "No."

"Well," I said, after an uncomfortably long moment passed between us, "I should be going. I've taken up enough of your time." I stood up and said, "Thank you for the shade and water."

Mrs. Reissman stood and retrieved her basket of cut flowers and the pruning shears and walked with me onto the lawn. I looked around again at the neat, well-groomed lawn and flowerbeds. "This is a lovely place," I said. "I can see why you enjoy spending time here. However, I noticed that the driveway I used is quite overgrown and in need of some trimming. Is there another entrance you use instead?"

It was a straightforward question and should have been easy to answer, but she seemed hesitant to respond. "I seldom go anywhere," she finally said, "I suppose the staff uses another driveway. I don't pay much attention to such things. Summer Rest is where I want to be," she said, smiling, "and until my Robert comes home, where I intend to stay."

"Yes, ma'am," I said. I extended my hand. Vanessa shook it gently. "Thank you for your hospitality." I turned and began walking back the way I had come, then, as if I had only just thought of it, I turned back and asked, "Does the name Sarah mean anything to you?"

Mrs. Reissman did not answer. I was about to repeat my question when she said, "I have an aunt named Sarah, and I had a best friend by that name when I was in high school. Why do you ask?"

Once again, I was conflicted over my desire to be honest and forthright and feeling the need to hold back a bit on the truth. I went for the latter and kept my answer vague. "I met a young girl named Sarah alongside the highway yesterday evening. It was this Sarah who pointed out your house to me across the lake. Do you know who she is?" I asked.

She took no time at all in answering me. "No," she said. "I've no idea who that could be."

Mrs. Reissman began rummaging through the flowers in her basket. She came up with a yellow rose and held it up for me to see. "Do you know what is symbolized by yellow spring flowers, Mr. Ryan?"

"No, ma'am," I said.

"Yellow spring flowers symbolize life, Mr. Ryan. I have cut these to go into a vase I keep on the table in my entryway to remind me of all those who have lost their lives fighting in this awful war. Please take this one and think of those who will never return to their homes and their loved ones."

"Thank you," I said, and took the flower from her. I looked at Mrs. Reissman for a moment, wondering about this elegant and strange woman, so much out of place on this secluded lakefront estate, seemingly unaware that the war she claimed her husband was fighting had ended more than a decade and a half ago. I wondered how this could be possible. Surely, she read the newspapers and listened to the radio and television. I wondered, too, about her husband. Where was he? Was he currently serving in the military? Could Mrs. Reissman merely be confused about the nature of her husband's deployment? I seemed to have more of a mystery on my hands now than when Sarah pointed the house out to me across the twilight lake.

"You do have a lovely home," I said, looking past her at the stately structure. "Thank you again for your hospitality." I turned and began walking toward my truck.

"Oh, Mr. Ryan," Mrs. Reissman called. I turned. "Do come by again sometime."

"I will," I said.

Chapter 4

I drove back out to the highway and turned toward home. I wanted to check on the fawn and give him a mid-day bottle. As I approached the spot where I met Sarah last evening, I saw that she was once again sitting on the birch log, her dress as yellow as the midday sun. She leaped to her feet as I pulled my pickup to the side of the road, and when I approached her, she immediately wrapped her thin arms around my waist and looked up at me with wide-eyed expectation.

"Hello, honey," I said and hugged her. She was as warm and real as any living person, and I had to remind myself that she was a spirit as intangible as a breath of air, though standing there and looking at her, she appeared as three-dimensional as me. I could even smell the aroma of lilac drifting up from her hair.

"Let's sit down," I said, and guided her to the birch log. I sat first, and Sarah took a seat beside me. She took the time to smooth her dress across her lap, and then she folded her tiny gloved hands primly in her lap and sat very erect as she looked anxiously at me. She displayed a refinement that is uncharacteristic in girls her age, and I surmised that she must have had a very proper upbringing for the short time she lived.

"I visited the house today," I said. Sarah's eyes opened wide when she heard this and a broad exuberant smile broke out on her face. She reached out and pulled my hands onto her lap and held them tightly, bouncing with excitement. "I spoke with the lady that lives there," I said. "Her name is Vanessa Reissman. Do you know her?" Sarah nodded vigorously and leaned toward me and wrapped her arms around me. I took her by the shoulders and held her at arm's length to look at her. "Who is Vanessa Reissman?" I asked.

She said nothing, but great tears began to well in her eyes. Her inability or unwillingness to speak was frustrating. I had no idea what she wanted or expected of me, but her reaction to my news made it clear that my brief encounter with Vanessa Reissman meant a great deal to her. She retook my hands and squeezed them tightly and looked into my eyes with singular intensity.

"What is it, honey," I asked. "What are you trying to tell me?"

Sarah let go of my hands and stood to face me. She closed her eyes and remained very still for several seconds, as if in deep concentration like an Olympic diver preparing to leap. After a few moments, she opened her eyes again, and I heard a sound like fabric ripping. It was an ugly noise that seemed to come from all around me, and at the same time from nowhere at all. I caught a whiff of ozone, sharp and pungent, and Sarah's visage began flickering, growing dim and transparent, and then rematerializing in rapid succession before fading again. She stuttered in and out of visibility very rapidly, as if she were having trouble maintaining visible form. A moment later, I was jolted from my fascination by a strange sensation on my flesh. It felt as if thousands of spiders were crawling over every square inch of my skin, and I thought that I had disturbed an insect nest by sitting on the log. I slapped frantically at my arms and the back of my neck until I realized there was nothing there. It was merely the fine hairs on my skin causing the prickling sensation, and for a moment, despite the clear sky, I wondered if lightning were about to strike.

I settled down and looked back at Sarah. She had begun to move, and the flickering of her now visible, now invisible form produced a strobe-like effect that made her movements seem as if her joints were somehow hinged improperly. She moved stiffly in a spasm of jerks and twitches, wavering like visible static. She began acting out a series of movements: touching her lips, shaking her head, pointing toward the huge white pine with the old scar near its base, all the while fading in and out like the picture on a television set receiving a weak signal.

The sun slipped behind a dense cloud, plunging us in deep shade that made her movements even more disturbing. Whatever energy or force made her visible to me, at times seemed to leave her, causing her to fade like dissipating mist. A great gust of wind bent the grass and whipped the treetops, and somewhere in the forest at my back, I heard the unmistakable sound of a tree splintering and crashing to the ground. And then, it was utterly still again.

Sarah's expression changed. Her eyes shot open, and she brought her arms up and grasped some invisible object before her, as if hanging on for dear life. Her small body began convulsing in a spasm of violent side-to-side motion;

her head lolled uncontrollably upon her neck. Her hat was suddenly thrown off by some unseen force, and her hair flew as if blown by a strong wind. She wore an expression of surprise and terror so heavy I thought my heart would collapse under its weight. It became a silent and terrified scream, and then Sarah crossed her forearms in front of her face, as if to ward off a blow.

I have seen mimes performing their silent art with great mastery of the craft, but the act Sarah performed for me was more convincing than any who had ever donned white face paint and a bowler hat. I tried to reach out to her, to somehow shield her from harm, but I was unable to move. It was as if I were waking while under the paralysis of a horrible nightmare, conscious of my body, but unable to command it.

All at once, Sarah's body was thrown forward at tremendous speed, as if some great force had shoved her violently from behind. She struck no visible barrier, nevertheless, her face distorted and flattened, her teeth shattered, and her lips and nose became nothing more than a pulp of flesh. An instant later, her upper body went limp and dangled from the waist at a grotesque angle, her mangled and bloody arms hanging limply at her sides like a marionette cut loose from her strings.

Mercifully, I could no longer see her face. It was shrouded by her hair which was soaked with blood and hanging like broken wings on either side of her head. The horrific image continued to flicker, the odor of ozone remained heavy on the air but now mingled with the smell of gasoline and hot motor oil.

I gasped and tried to take a breath, but it was as if my lungs had filled with concrete. I had no voice. All that came from me was a weak, protracted moan. The world went out of focus, and I felt a sinking sensation as if I was standing on a frozen lake and the ice had suddenly dropped out from under me. I blinked my eyes and gasped and slid off the log onto my knees. The jolt got my breathing going again, and I filled my lungs with air. Great shuddering sobs rushed out of me and my vision blurred with tears.

I felt Sarah's hand on my head, and I slipped my arms around her slender waist and buried my face in the folds of her dress and sobbed. I don't know how long I remained that way, but presently, I became aware of a voice calling to me from the direction of the highway. Sarah patted me tenderly on the back of my head and helped me back onto the log, then sat next to me, holding onto my hand as I got myself under control. A car had pulled onto the gravel shoulder of the highway behind my truck, and the driver had rolled down his window.

"Are you alright?" the man asked.

I couldn't speak. I couldn't form proper words. I just stammered out some unintelligible sound in reply to his question. I'm sure I was coming across like some lunatic sitting alongside the highway babbling and crying.

"Do you need help?" he asked.

I took a few deep breaths and wiped my eyes. Sarah squeezed my other hand comfortingly, and I recovered sufficiently to respond. "No. I'm fine." I said, not knowing what to tell this concerned passer-by.

"Are you sure?" he asked.

"Yes. I just felt a little nauseous," I lied, "so I pulled over so I wouldn't be sick in my truck. I'll be fine in a minute or two." I took a sideways glance at Sarah sitting beside me on the log.

"Well," he said, "I hate to leave you sitting out here all alone if you're not well. I can drive you somewhere if you'd like."

He couldn't see her. She was right there in my peripheral vision, and I could feel her gloved hand, smooth and cool, holding onto mine, but he could see only me seated on the birch log.

"I'm fine," I assured him. "I'm just going to sit here for a while and then drive myself home. I don't live far from here."

"Are you sure?" he asked.

"Yes," I said. "I'm feeling better. Something I ate isn't sitting right with me. I'm just going to take another moment or two before heading home."

He nodded at me, and as I watched him drive away, I felt Sarah's hand slip out of mine. I looked to my left, and she was gone, but she left behind the aroma of lilac.

Chapter 5

I turned into my driveway and saw Doctor Rayburn's truck parked in front of my garage. I went inside and found the good doctor seated on a wooden crate feeding a bottle of milk replacer to a very hungry fawn. Doctor Rayburn looked up at me smiling. "He seems to be doing fine," he said.

I turned an empty five-gallon bucket upside down to use as a stool and sat next to him. "He sure has a good appetite," I said. "I'm glad to see him taking the bottle so well."

The little buck was standing tripod fashion with his injured leg lifted slightly off the floor as he sucked hungrily at the bottle. The little flag of his tail spun like a pinwheel in a windstorm. A stream of saliva and milk replacer ran from his muzzle. His frenzied feeding was so comical I couldn't help laughing out loud. For a moment, I completely forgot the horrible one-act play Sarah had performed for me only minutes ago.

The bottle was collapsing in upon itself as the fawn tried to coax more milk replacer from it. Doctor Rayburn had to forcibly pull it from the fawn's mouth, and he nearly fell over backward when it came free. We made a hasty retreat from the garage, pulling the bottom half of the door closed behind us so that the fawn wouldn't wander outside. It wouldn't due for him to make a break for the tree line before I was sure he would survive.

We went inside my cabin, and Doctor Rayburn cleaned up in my bathroom while I washed the empty bottle in hot soapy water and set it in my drying rack. Doctor Rayburn came into the kitchen drying his hands on a towel, and I asked him if he could spare a few minutes to talk. He said he didn't have an appointment for an hour, so I took two cans of RC Cola from my refrigerator, and we went outside to sit in the shade.

I have a pair of old metal lawn chairs that I bought for a dollar each at a garage sale last summer. They were painted an insipid shade of yellow, but I spent an entire day sanding them down and repainting them bright red. They were cheerful to look at and cool to sit in, if not left directly in the sun.

We pulled the chairs deep into the shade of a big maple and sat looking toward the garage while we sipped the RCs. I hadn't seen the doe today, and I was feeling anxious about her giving up on her baby and moving on. I said as much to Doctor Rayburn.

The doctor fished a pipe from his left breast pocket and a pouch of apple-scented tobacco from his right. He went to work filling and lighting his pipe, and between puffs, he said, "I wouldn't worry too much about it, Tommy. Wild animals have a strong mothering instinct and will do almost anything within their power to take care of their young. I've heard tales of does taking on full-grown wolves to keep their fawns from harm. They can practically walk on their rear legs while slashing out with their forehooves when forced to fight." He smoked in silence for a moment and then said, "She knows her baby is in your garage. I think she'll stay close for a while yet, a few days anyway."

I was relieved to hear it, but I knew I wouldn't fully relax until I spotted the doe again.

The day was unusually warm for early May, but there was a gentle breeze, and it was pleasant sitting in the shade, smelling the aroma of Doctor Rayburns's pipe, and looking out across the yard toward the forest and the garage. The songbirds had returned to the Northwoods, and the trees were full of what my mother called "nature's glee club." I took a long drink from my can of RC. It was cold and felt good going down. Doctor Rayburn was slumped low in his chair with his head back and his eyes closed. He had a contented little grin on his face. We sat in companionable silence for a time listening to the chorus of songbirds.

"Doctor Rayburn, can I ask you a question?" I finally asked.

"Yes," he said, without opening his eyes.

"Do you recall any traffic accidents on the highway at the bottom of Eagle Bluff?"

"Yes," he said, keeping his eyes closed. "I can think of a few. That hill gets pretty slippery in the winter. There's a lot of deer that cross right in through there too, and someone's always knocking into them."

I was quiet for a moment, trying to decide how best to ask him for specifics without having to explain why I was asking. Doctor Rayburn is a respected man around here, and I value his friendship and his opinion of me as well. The last thing I wanted was for him to think that I had gone over the edge with hallucinations. I decided to creep up on the topic and hope he wouldn't see anything more in it than casual interest.

"Do you recall any fatalities?" I asked.

He didn't respond right away, and I wasn't sure if he was thinking or sleeping. I was about to repeat my questions when he said, "It seems to me that there have been a couple of fatalities right in through that area. It's been quite a while though, and I can't recall anything specific. Why do you ask?"

There it was; the question I was hoping he wouldn't ask. What was I going to tell him? *Well, Doctor, it's like this; I've been talking to a dead girl who haunts that stretch of highway, only the conversation has been sort of one-sided. She wants me to do something for her, but she can't, or won't, talk to me, and I have no idea what she wants, so I was hoping you could tell me.*

My dear mother strived to instill within me a propensity for honesty, and I always try to honor my mother, so I decided to go with a half-truth. "I was out of my truck at the bottom of the grade yesterday," I said, "and my foot struck something buried in the dead grass. I pulled it out, and it was one of those little crosses people place alongside the road to mark the site where somebody died; usually, it's a car wreck."

Doctor Rayburn opened his eyes and looked at me. "I've seen a few of those here and there," he said, "but I don't recall ever seeing one at the bottom of Eagle Bluff."

"Well," I said, "somebody placed one out there. I found it tangled in dead grass. I figure it got knocked over by a snowplow."

The expression on his face became somewhat sorrowful, and he shook his head slightly. "Those little crosses are such sad memorials. There's something about a car wreck that's particularly miserable," he said as he sat up straight in his chair. "Maybe it's because of the unexpected and violent nature of a crash. You know what I mean; you're just driving along on your way to visit a friend or maybe going to church or work, and in the blink of an eye, your existence has come to an end. You're done making history. There's no more future to become your past."

He leaned forward and knocked his pipe against the bottom of his shoe, dislodging the burnt tobacco. "It's either arbitrary or purposefully ordained by the great power that runs this universe," he said. "Either way, it gives me the willies."

I sat quietly for a moment, giving his words proper consideration and staring into my can of RC as if the answers to my mystery could be found within its depths. Finally, I said, "It wasn't a recent wreck. The cross had been there for quite some time. It was in pretty bad shape, but whoever made it had painted it white and written on it. It was badly faded, but I was able to make out the name Sarah and the year 1948."

Doctor Rayburn gazed across the yard at the tall fir trees and watched their severely tapered tops swaying gently in the breeze. "Sarah and 1948," he repeated. He bit the inside of his lip thoughtfully and said, "That was thirteen years ago. I moved up here from Madison to open my practice in the fall of 1948. Could have happened earlier in the year, and I wouldn't have heard about it."

"That's most likely what happened," I said. "Still, curiosity has got the better part of me, and I'd like to try to find out about that crash. You know a lot of people around here," I said, "who should I talk to? Who might know what happened back then?"

Doctor Rayburn gave it some thought and said, "If I were you, I'd drive into town and stop by the library to have a look through the old newspapers. They keep them in an archive in the basement. A fatal car crash is sure to have made it into the papers. Talk to Edna Rollins; she's the head librarian." He winked at me and said, "She was born about two years before Moses, but she has lived around here all her life. If anyone can help you, she can."

"That's a good idea, sir. Thanks."

"Hey," Doctor Rayburn said. I looked and saw that he was pointing towards the trees. The doe was barely visible as she stood in the deep shadow of the forest watching us.

Chapter 6

I drove the six miles into the town where I had grown up and pulled into the parking lot of the Joshua Falls Public Library. My mother sold our house and moved in with her sister in Iron Mountain, Michigan shortly after I moved into Ted Morgan's cabin. I work in Alibi, which is on the Wisconsin side of the border only a few miles from Iron Mountain, so I tend to do all of my shopping there on the days when I visit with my mother and aunt. With no real connection any longer to "The Falls," as everyone referred to it, it had been about five years since I last visited the public library, and as I entered its cavernous vestibule, a wave of nostalgia hit me.

I stood stock-still taking in the familiar sight of the heavy oak doors with their wide push bars and gleaming brass kick plates. The vestibule had tiled floors, a high plaster ceiling, and solid oak woodwork polished smooth by years of cleaning. A community bulletin board hung on the wall to my right, and I took a moment to read the notices posted there. I finished perusing the announcements and then strode to the far end of the vestibule while listening to my echoing footfalls.

I pushed through the double doors and entered the library and breathed in the dry and slightly dusty odor of book paper. Nothing at all seemed to have changed. The familiar oak tables were still strategically arranged in double rows of three before the librarian's desk, no doubt to better facilitate shushing whenever the level of conversation rose above a whisper. To the right of the tables, just where I remembered them to be, stood the three multi-drawered wooden cabinets containing the library's card catalog. The checkout counter, with its carved wooden plaque reading LENDING DESK, remained firmly anchored to the floor on the left side of the reading tables. Everything appeared virtually unchanged, right down to its rack of date stamps, the assortment of pens and pencils, and pads of scratch paper.

I looked to my right where a long window spanned the library's east wall and walked over to it. The marble windowsill was as cool as a fudge maker's stone table. I leaned on it and gazed out across Third Street at the ornate bandstand standing at the center of City Park. The familiar sight instantly erased the years that had passed since I had last looked out this very window as a boy. Again, a wave of nostalgia crashed into me.

I had been just ten years old when black lung took my father from my mother and me. The last months of his life had played out in a sick bed hacking sooty phlegm into towels and shriveling from a vibrant man of one hundred and eighty pounds to just over ninety. A sallow, wheezing skeleton had replaced the father who had come home every night from his job at the charcoal briquette factory in Kingsford and sipped RC Cola with me on our front steps.

Our conversations had moved from our shaded front porch to a chair next to his bed in a small guestroom just off our kitchen that my mother had converted to a sickroom. His exciting tales of deer hunts and canoe excursions down the Menominee River had deteriorated into unintelligible ramblings rasped out between strangled bouts of coughing.

After a time, when even the act of speaking had become too taxing for him, our conversations ceased altogether. During those long, unbearable days, I would sit quietly with him while I did my homework before supper. Sometimes I would read to him from one of my library books, and on a good day, we could even manage a game of checkers played with his bedside stand placed between us.

I wanted to be there during the early stages of my father's decline. I wanted to give what little comfort a ten-year-old boy could, but as he inched ever closer to death, the sight of his waxy pallor, the knife-like blade of his nose jutting away from his hollow-cheeked face, and the stench that rose from his sweat-slicked skin eventually drove me away, and I steadfastly refused even to enter the room.

My mother tried to compel me to sit with him by appealing to my sense of shame at abandoning my father during his time of need. But the guilt I felt at her cajoling was nothing compared with my fear and distaste of the man who now looked to me more like the scarecrow propped up on the pole in our neighbor's garden than the man who taught me to ride my bike and throw a football. In spite of my mother's coaxing, I held my ground and stubbornly refused to step one foot inside his room. I had convinced myself that it would be when I was with him that the inevitable would happen. I would look up from my homework to find his lifeless, unseeing eyes staring at me, as if to fix within his soul's memory one last look at his son before entering into eternity. That was a memory I could not bear to own, and so, when my mother was not in the kitchen, I would sidle up to his open door and, without so much as a glance inside, quietly close it.

During my father's illness, my mother supplemented what little money they had in their bank account with part-time work at the Woodsman Café out on Town Line Road. Their savings gave out at about the same time my father's life gave out, and there had been no death benefit from the factory and no life insurance. My mother's part-time hours soon became full time. Most days, her shift didn't end until two hours after the end of the school day, and on those days, I would walk home to an empty house and fix a peanut butter sandwich to eat at the kitchen table while I did my homework.

On one particularly dreary November afternoon, with sleet hissing against the little window over the sink, my concentration was interrupted by a sound that made gooseflesh break out on my arms and caused the fine hairs on the back of my neck to prickle. It was the sound of the door of my dead father's sick room, which I carefully closed before I sat down to my homework, slowly creaking open on its hinges. Even more disturbing were the sounds of wet, labored breathing, squeaking bedsprings, and bare feet shuffling on the worn linoleum floor.

I couldn't move. I didn't dare turn around and risk a look. I just sat there frozen with fear, incapable of fleeing until I felt a bony hand fall on my shoulder, at which point I fled. I snatched up my books, even as I was rising from my chair, and ran straight to the public library, sans coat, and from that day forward, the library was my after-school refuge. Warm, well-lit and well-populated, it was my sanctuary, a place where I could escape the cold of winter and my certainty that the door to the little room just off our kitchen was standing open.

I spent a great deal of time at the library during the years following my father's death. I did my homework at one of the long tables in front of the librarian's desk, and any extra time afterward was spent reading outdoor adventure stories written by the likes of Jack London and Jim Kjelgaard, while sitting in a chair pulled up close to the steam radiator that ran below the library's long window. In the heat of the summer, its thick brick walls kept it as cool as an air-conditioned room. In the wintertime, it was a bulwark standing against the howling snowstorms that frequently battered Joshua Falls.

Fair weather or foul, I barely noticed the hours passing as I devoured books like *White Fang* and *Big Red*. On one occasion, I weathered a particularly severe Nor'easter by reading halfway through *The Yearling* before my mother stopped by to retrieve me after work at the Woodsman.

I left my memories to hang in the air over the bandstand and pulled myself away from the window. I walked to the checkout counter to speak with the librarian. She was a youngish-looking woman with thick glasses and a prominent overbite. She was busy checking in a sizeable stack of books and didn't look up at me when I approached. I waited patiently, not wanting to interrupt her work, and after a minute, she closed the cover on the last book in the stack, looked up at me over her reading glasses, and asked if she could help me.

"I'd like to speak with Edna Rollins," I said, "if she's available."

The young woman whose name was Janet—according to the name badge protruding from under her wide collar—said, "Just a moment," and walked across the room to an office door in the west wall. She knocked and then walked in leaving the door slightly ajar. A moment later, she came back out followed by a severe-looking woman who appeared to be in her eighties. She was wearing a floral print dress and thick-soled shoes. I know I should have recognized her from my days here as a boy, but I didn't. How many young boys take note of elderly librarians?

"I am Edna Rollins. May I help you?" she asked as she approached and stepped behind the desk.

"Yes, ma'am," I said. "My name is Tommy Ryan. A friend told me that it might be possible to look at old copies of the *Falls Herald*. He said you keep them archived here."

"Yes," she said. "We keep all of the local newspapers and copies of the *Wisconsin State Journal* and *The Milwaukee Journal* going back many years. What period interests you?"

"Actually, ma'am, I was hoping you could help me narrow it down. I know the year is 1948, but I am not sure which month. My friend suggested that you may be familiar with the event I want to research and be able to help me find the specific newspaper; if you have the time, that is. I don't want to be a bother if you have other things to do."

"Well, Mister Ryan," she said, coming around the desk, "I think I can spare some time to help you. Tell me, who is this friend of yours?"

"His name is Michael Rayburn. He's a veterinarian with a farm practice in the area."

"Oh, I know Doctor Rayburn. He stops in here now and again. He is fond of the Western genre. He has fairly exhausted our supply of Louis L'Amours and Zane Greys. His favorite is *Riders of the Purple Sage*," she said, and gestured down an aisle between two long rows of bookshelves. "I haven't seen the doctor for a while. How is he?" she asked as we began walking.

"He's fine, ma'am," I said. "He keeps busy."

"Well, you tell him hello for me and mention that I have acquired several copies of *Wild West Weekly* dating back to 1908. He's free to read them, though he'll have to read them here and handle them carefully."

"I'll be sure to let him know," I said as we reached a heavy oak door set into the wall in a dimly lit corner at the back of the library.

"We keep the back copies of all periodicals in the basement," she said. "They're stored in plastic wrappers to protect them from damp and dust." At that, she produced a ring of keys from a pocket in her dress and slipped one into the lock. She opened the door and reached in and flipped on a light illuminating a long flight of steps painted industrial gray with a black rubber runner down the center. "Come along, Mister Ryan," she said, and started down the stairs. At the bottom, Mrs. Rollins flipped another light switch.

We were in a cavernous room whose dimensions were impossible to determine, as the long, block walls, also painted with thick industrial gray enamel, disappeared beyond the spill of the overhead lights. Tall metal shelves stood back to back in the center of the room and more lined the walls as far as the overhead lights would reveal. It was a room I would not want to be locked in during a power failure. There did not appear to be any windows set into the tall walls, and I could hear no sound other than those we were making. The air carried a faint musty odor mingled with the scent of dust and paper.

"Now, Mister Ryan," Mrs. Rollins said, walking deep into the rows of shelves, "you mentioned the *Falls Herald* for 1948, correct?"

"Yes, ma'am," I said.

She cast an eye over myriad cardboard cartons placed neatly on the shelves. She moved up and down the rows with her hands clasped in the small of her back looking like a military officer inspecting her troops. Glints of white light flashed off her eyeglasses when her gaze went to the higher shelves. I could see that each carton was marked with a bold script identifying the periodical and the years of publication contained within each box. She had found the boxes containing the *Falls Herald* and was busy scanning dates. After a long moment, she proclaimed, "1948. Here we are."

I stepped forward and looked where she was pointing. There were two cartons on a high shelf dated 1948. "I'll let you take those down for me," she said, and stepped back to give me space.

I pulled down both boxes, and Mrs. Rollins directed me to carry them to a long table against the wall beneath the staircase. She turned on two desk lamps and flooded the tabletop with light, then opened the boxes. There were two heavy oak swivel desk chairs on casters, and we both sat down. "Now tell me," she said, "what is this event you want to read about?"

There was no sense in reinventing the wheel, so I repeated what I had told Doctor Rayburn about finding the old, faded cross bearing Sarah's name and the date 1948 and my desire to learn more about what must have been a fatal car crash on that spot along the highway. It was nothing more than curiosity, morbid though it may be.

Mrs. Rollins was quiet for a long moment, then something like recognition slid onto her face, and she said, "I think I remember that accident." Another pause and she said more firmly, "Yes, I do. It was tragic, just tragic. A little girl was killed on the spot and her mother seriously injured." She began rummaging through one of the boxes and pulled out several rolled newspapers. She carefully removed the plastic cover from one and spread it out on the table. It was dated July 7th.

"The *Falls Herald* is a weekly that comes out every Wednesday," she said. "Let's see what we can find in here."

Mrs. Rollins began turning pages, her eyes scanning the rows of print looking for headlines that may relate to the accident. After turning every page in wide, careful arcs, she set the July 7th edition aside and slipped the previous week's paper from its plastic protector and said, "It was not in the winter, I can recall that much," she said. "If memory serves me, that accident occurred in the early summer or maybe the spring. That narrows the search a bit."

Engrossed in the task of locating a story about the crash, Mrs. Rollins had been speaking without looking directly at me. After a moment, she looked up at me over her glasses and said, "Oh dear, what's the matter with me? Let's have you start with June," she said. "After all, this is your research project." She handed me four plastic wrapped weekly issues for June of 1948, and I started in on the issue dated June 2nd.

In 1948, the *Falls Herald* was no different than any other small-town newspaper. Local news and advertising took up the most space, but room was also provided for columns devoted to everything from whose grandchildren came for a visit with whom, to national news and sports reporting. Under a column titled "National Week in Review," there was a story describing the devastation of a town in Oregon named Vanport, which had nearly been destroyed after a dike on the Columbia River failed. Fifteen people had been killed and thousands were left homeless. In the same column, under the subheading "Sporting News," Tommy Lasorda, playing for the Schenectady Blue Jays, had an amazing twenty-five strikeouts in fifteen innings against the Amsterdam Rugmakers, and Mauri Rose had won the Indianapolis 500.

Sadness came over me as I scanned these stories. Had my father not been so sick when these events occurred, we would have likely talked about them, perhaps while tossing a baseball in our front yard or while sitting on our big front porch in the evening after he had come home from work. In the spring of 1948, there had been no casual conversations about notable events, local or national. It had been all my mother and I could do to take care of my father and keep the utility bills paid. There had been no baseball games playing on the radio and no commentary from my father, as he no longer joined us at the breakfast table to read his newspaper.

I looked up from the June 2nd issue to find Mrs. Rollins returning the July issues to their box and starting in on August. I returned the June 2nd issue to its plastic wrapper, set it aside, and worked my way through the issues for the weeks of June 9, 16, and 23. I found nothing and was about to move on to the newspapers for May when I realized that I had not checked all issues for June. There had been five Wednesdays in June of 1948 and the final week's issue came out on June 30th. I found it in the carton and slipped it from its protective wrapper. The story was just below the fold.

"Mrs. Rollins," I said, spreading the paper out flat on the table before me, "I think I've found what I am searching for." She laid aside the paper she was scanning and slid her chair close to mine. "This is the June 30th edition," I said, gesturing at the front-page story under a headline which read:

One Killed One Injured in Eagle Bluff Collision
By Dennis Cain

Tragically, a little girl died yesterday, and her mother was seriously injured in a one-car collision along State Road 141 at the base of Eagle Bluff seven miles west of Joshua Falls in Alibi Township. Vanessa Reissman, later identified as Mrs. Robert Reissman, was driving her 1947 Ford Pilot with her eight-year-old daughter, Sarah Marie Reissman, riding in the front passenger seat. For an undetermined reason, the Ford left the road, striking a large pine tree on the east side of the highway. The little girl was partially ejected from the car, and the mother knocked unconscious.

A passing motorist, Mr. James Osbourne of Joshua Falls, happened upon the scene and attempted to render aid, but the little girl was found to have already died. A second motorist on the scene quickly drove three miles to the nearest home with a telephone and called the police while Mr. Osbourne stayed with Mrs. Reissman. Marinette County Sheriff's Deputy, Aaron Cooper, was the first police officer on the scene. He administered lifesaving first aid to Vanessa Reissman and is credited, along with James Osbourne and the unnamed motorist who went for help, with saving her life. "I have never seen anything like it," Deputy Cooper said, visibly shaken. "I have a little girl of my own, and to see that little girl halfway through the windshield the way she was, well, it just really gets to you." Ambulance personnel transported Mrs. Reissman to Joshua Falls Medical Center where her condition is said to be serious. The Marinette County Coroner removed the body of Sarah Reissman from the scene, and a wrecker from Johnson's Auto Salvage towed the Ford. There is no information yet as to what caused the accident. Mrs. Reissman is the wife of Captain Robert Reissman who is serving with the 6th Army in the Philippines and has been listed as missing in action since the Lingayen Gulf invasion in January of 1945. Robert Reissman is the only child of now diseased Calvin and Mary Reissman of Chicago, a well-known family with ties to finance and banking. Vanessa Reissman and her daughter have been residing at the family estate in rural Alibi Township. Funeral services for Sarah Marie Reissman will be announced.

I finished reading and leaned back in my chair and said, "Well, there it is."

"Yes," Mrs. Rollins said as she removed her reading glasses and allowed them to dangle around her neck. "I remember now. It was horrible. That sweet little girl killed and her mother gravely injured. Tragic," she said, shaking her head.

"Yes, it is," I said. "Mrs. Rollins, do you remember what happened in the days and weeks after the accident? Were there any other articles, any information about the little girl's funeral or the mother's recovery?"

"I really can't say with any certainty, Mr. Ryan. That story," she said, gesturing toward the open newspaper on the table between us, "triggered my recollection of the accident, but that's where it ends for me. That was well over a decade ago." She stood up and said, "I have to return to my duties upstairs, but you are welcome to stay down here and search for later issues. You may come across another article."

"Thank you," I said. "I think I will."

"Take all the time you need," she said as she turned to leave. "Please be sure to return each paper to its protective sleeve and return the carton to its place on the shelf. Come on up when you are finished and make sure the door locks behind you."

"Yes, ma'am. Thank you," I said.

"I guess now you know the story behind that little cross you found along the highway," Mrs. Rollins said as she walked toward the stairway.

It was true. I had indeed learned something very important: Sarah was the daughter of the elegant woman I had spoken with this morning at the house named Summer Rest; the woman who, when I asked her, denied knowing a little girl named Sarah.

I spent the next hour looking for follow up stories relating to the crash, Sarah's funeral, and her mother's recovery, but I found nothing. The post-war years were a busy time with much more important events happening every day all around the globe. Perhaps the death of a little girl along a rural Wisconsin highway didn't warrant a follow-up. Whatever the reason, I determined that I would find no other useful information in the archives.

I returned all newspapers to the carton except the July 30th edition. Before I put it away, I took a small notebook and a pencil from my shirt pocket and jotted down a few details from the article. I made a note of the reporter's name, the name of the wrecker service that towed the car from the scene, the police officer, and the name of the good Samaritan who stopped to render aid. It wasn't much to go on, but it was a start.

I went back up to the library, thanked Mrs. Rollins again, and walked out to my truck. It was just after one o'clock, and I decided to stop by the newspaper office to see if I could locate and speak with Dennis Cain, assuming he was still with the paper. The article filled in some of the blanks for me, but for every question answered, there was one that remained unanswered. It was evident that Vanessa Reissman had recovered from her injuries and returned to Summer Rest, but why did she believe that her husband, who was missing in action at the time of the accident, was still fighting in the Philippines? Could her confusion be the result of the injuries she sustained in the crash? Was this also the reason why she denied knowing her daughter when I asked if the name Sarah meant anything to her?

As for Sarah, what exactly did she want from me? Why was she haunting the place where she had died, and what would it take to get her to move on, if moving on was what she was supposed to do? Did she even want to move on? As I climbed into my truck, I hoped the answers to my questions would be gleaned from a conversation with Dennis Cain.

Chapter 7

As it turned out, Dennis Cain was still with the *Joshua Falls Herald* but no longer working as a reporter. He had purchased the paper in 1955 when the former owner, Oliver Kessler, retired. When I told him that I was looking into the accident that killed Sarah Reissman and critically injured her mother, Dennis seemed pleased to help and invited me back to his office where he took a seat behind a desk overflowing with clutter. He listened to my story about finding the roadside cross and wanting to satisfy my curiosity about the accident and offered to pull the story he had written back in 1948.

"I've just come from reading it at the library," I explained. "I was hoping you could shed additional light on what had occurred in the days and months after the accident and why I couldn't find any follow-up stories."

"Well," he said, leaning back in his chair and removing the half-specs he wore far down on his nose, "I wanted to do a follow-up piece, but Oliver Kessler didn't think it worthy of additional ink."

"That seems odd," I said. "I would think the death of a little girl and the serious injuring of her mother would be big news around here."

Dennis sat quietly and appeared to be weighing his words before doling them out. After a moment, he leaned forward, folded his hands on his desk, and said, "I hate to badmouth anybody. Oliver Kessler hired me when I had zero experience as a reporter. He taught me most of what I know about the job. When it came his time to get out of the business, the buyout deal he gave me on the paper made it possible for me to take over. I owe him a lot, but the truth is Oliver Kessler was the worst kind of anti-Semite, and he couldn't care one iota about the tragic death of a little Jewish girl."

I had to think about that for a moment. I had no idea Sarah was Jewish. I know there are anti-Semites living in America who hate Jews as much as the Nazis, but I hadn't considered that there could be any living here in my little hometown, and I shared this thought with Dennis.

"Oh," he said emphatically, "you'd be surprised how many anti-Semites there were about these parts back then, and you didn't have to go farther than the Woodsman Café to find them either. Most mornings, you'd find Ollie drinking coffee and shaking dice with some of the most hate-filled men you could ever meet. These were the good ole boys that ran businesses and sat in church pews and even taught in the schools. And now and then, some of those old boys got up to mischief too, you know, busting windows in the middle of the night or painting swastikas on houses and businesses. I remember one time this poor Jewish kid got the crap kicked out of him walking back from a date with his high school sweetheart. They put him in the hospital for a week."

"So that's why there were no follow up stories on the accident? Mr. Kessler didn't want to generate sympathy for the Reissman family because they were Jewish?" I asked.

"There was that," he said, leaning forward and folding his hands on top of a desk blotter scribbled with notes and doodles, "but his decisions about content were also related to the rather grandiose ideas he had about his little weekly."

"I don't understand," I said.

"Kessler was an immigrant who came here with his family from Germany in 1921 to escape the economic hardships after the end of World War I. His father had run one of the largest papers in Berlin, and Kessler had grown up enjoying a goodly amount of prestige in the community and no small amount of pride in the family business. Upon arriving in the United States, the best his father could do was land a job as a typesetter for a third-rate paper in Upstate New York. Oliver confided to me one day that it was a personal embarrassment for him to see his father reduced to a mere laborer in a business where he had once been a king. You see, there was also an anti-German sentiment in America as the result of the recently ended war."

Dennis paused and took a cigar from a box on his desk and, after offering one to me, which I declined, lit it with a wooden match and puffed it into life. He picked a bit of tobacco from the tip of his tongue and rocked back in his chair again before going on with his story.

"Talking about it one day, Kessler told me that rather than stay in New York and waste away in Alexandria Bay— that was the little town were his family had settled—he struck out on his own and headed west. He ended up right here and landed a job with this paper in 1924, though at that time it was called the *Joshua Falls Call.* Within ten years, Kessler owned the paper, renamed it, and had big plans for growing it into a much larger enterprise. The depression put an end to those big plans and Kessler struggled simply to keep the paper afloat for many years. The Depression lasted much longer than most people realize. It took World War Two to end it finally. Eventually, Kessler admitted to himself that he was never going to be the owner of anything more than a small-town weekly."

Dennis paused in his narrative, rocked forward, and opened a desk drawer low on his right side. He came up with a half-full bottle of bourbon. "Time for my afternoon pick-me-up," he said. "Can I pour you one?"

I declined, and he splashed a small measure into a tumbler.

Dennis downed the bourbon and went on with his story. "Almost as much as Kessler hated the idea of running a rinky-dink hometown rag, he hated even more what passed for local news in those days. I remember him telling me once that if he had to print one more story about some old blue hair's grandchildren coming for a visit or which band was playing down at the Elks Club or report the minutes of the town council meeting, he was going to put a gun to his head. He kept one too; right here is this desk drawer. It was one of those Lugers the Krauts are so fond of."

"Then it would seem to me that a fatal car crash would have been big news from Mr. Kessler's viewpoint," I said.

"I agree with you," Dennis said, "but there was so much going on back then in the years immediately following the war that Oliver hated to devote any more space to the daily goings-on of this little hamlet than what was necessary. Traffic accidents, even fatal ones, didn't rate much reporting and, considering he was a dyed-in-the-wool Jew-hater, I'm surprised the crash made it into the paper at all."

He polished off another shot of bourbon and said, "Old Ollie wanted to pattern the paper after the likes of the *Chicago Tribune* or the *Milwaukee State Journal.* He wanted the big stories, but we're way up here in the Great White North, and it was just Oliver and me in those days. He had me selling advertising and covering the local stuff, and he filled the rest of the paper with world news he pulled off the wire services."

Dennis poured yet another shot and gestured in my direction with the bottle. I shook my head, and he returned it to his desk drawer. I felt like I had taken up enough of his time and stood to go. "Well, that explains why I couldn't find anything more on the accident," I said. "It's too bad. I would like to have learned more about what happened afterward with Vanessa Reissman. I don't suppose you heard about the extent of her injuries and how long it took her to recover?"

"Just a minute," Dennis said, and got up from his chair. He walked to a pair of louvered accordion doors set into the end wall of his office and pulled them open, revealing a closet stacked floor to ceiling with cardboard boxes, each labeled with dates scrawled in heavy black ink. About two-thirds of the way to the bottom, he pulled a carton marked 1945 to 1950 and carried it over and set it atop the clutter on his desk.

I watched him sift through file folders, legal pads, and notebooks, inspecting the handwritten information on each and muttering, "No, not this one. No, no," until he finally pulled a small spiral-bound notebook from the box and said, "Here it is." He looked at me and said, "Take a seat again. Maybe this will help you."

I reclaimed my chair and waited as he flipped past several pages. Without looking at me, he said, "The reporter in me, more specifically the reporter in me who's afraid of lawsuits and subpoenas, makes it his habit to save everything for many, many years. I never know when it will be needed to refresh my memory for a follow-up story or if I'm called into court. That can happen, and I don't want to get caught with my pants down around my ankles. Anyway, this is the notebook I was carrying back when the accident occurred. These are my notes about the accident. I used this to write the story you read."

He grabbed the back of his chair and pulled it around to my side of the desk, then sat next to me and laid the notebook where we could both look at it. "I wasn't at the scene of the accident," he said. "I didn't even know it had occurred until I heard the sirens heading up to the hospital." A sheepish look came over his face, and he said, "I know how that sounds, ambulance chaser and all, but it's how we knew something had happened. When I heard sirens, I made a point to head up to the hospital and check it out. Most of the time, it was a heart attack, or a little kid hit by a car, but that time, it was Mrs. Reissman."

I looked at his notebook but couldn't make out much of his handwriting. "You're going to have to translate this for me," I said. "I never learned to read hieroglyphics."

Dennis picked up his notebook and studied his undisciplined scrawl for a moment and then said, "I got to the hospital at about 11:30, just after Mrs. Reissman was wheeled into the emergency room." He stopped referring to his notes and looked at me and said, "Looking at this notebook brings it all back, and I remember quite a bit from that day. I remember hanging out by the intake nurse's desk until the ambulance driver came back out of the ER. His name was Jack Koepp. He was a regular driver back then—doesn't live around here anymore, I think he moved down to Portage a few years ago—but he was always pretty good about talking to me, so I followed him outside to the ambulance and asked him for details."

Dennis looked at his notebook again and flipped a page. I watched as his eyes sorted information and discarded unimportant tidbits. After a moment, he looked at me and said, "Here it is," and began reading: "JK arrived on scene approx. 11:15 a.m., observed 1947 Ford Pilot/black, wedged nose first into big pine. Windshield shattered on passenger side. Dashboard and hood covered in blood. Sheriff's deputy and unknown man tending to unconscious female driver. Small girl protruding through windshield. Yellow dress, a lot of blood. JK observed massive head trauma on girl, knew she was deceased but checked to confirm. Moved on to unconscious adult female who also displayed head trauma. Adult female was breathing. Serious lacerations on face and scalp. Possible chest wounds. Steering column bent at severe angle. Placed cervical collar and oxygen on subject and transported to JF hospital."

Dennis flipped a page or two, then flipped back and said, "The sheriff's deputy was named Aaron Cooper. He's no longer with the county. He retired a few years ago and moved down to Florida. He showed up at the hospital about an hour after the ambulance brought in Vanessa Reissman. I remember very well what he told me.

"Cooper said he was about eight miles west on the highway when he got the call about the accident. It only took him a few minutes to get there, and when he pulled up, he saw a man holding a bloody cloth against the forehead of an unconscious woman who was leaning at a severe angle in the driver's seat of a black Ford that had piled into a big pine. He ran over to the car and nearly lost his breakfast when he saw a little girl hanging out of the windshield by the waist. According to Cooper, she was impaled on shards of glass that remained in the windshield frame. He said her face had been ruined by the impact with the glass, and her hair was soaked in blood and 'hanging down on both sides of her face like dark red curtains.' The deputy said that the little girl's arms had gone through the glass with her head and they were hanging down on the car's hood. I'll never forget the way he described her. He said she looked like a 'marionette cut loose from its strings.'"

The mental image I formed as Dennis spoke was astonishingly vivid. I had witnessed it first-hand earlier at the crash scene, compliments of Sarah. Dennis looked up from his notes and must have seen a distressed look on my face because he asked me if I wanted that bourbon after all. I told him no and asked him what else he had found out that day.

"Well," he said, turning his attention back to his notebook, "later in the day, I was able to find out more about the extent of Vanessa Reissman's injuries. She had broken several ribs and suffered internal injuries when she hit the steering wheel. She managed to avoid a serious neck injury when she hit the windshield but received several deep lacerations to her face that would need cosmetic surgery to repair. I remember thinking that considering what happened to her daughter, the mother was lucky, not considering the grief she would experience once she learned that her little girl was dead."

I said nothing as I thought about the woman I sat with on the front porch of the big house she referred to as "Summer Rest."

"Tommy."

There had been no indication of scars anywhere, no deformity of any kind. Her face was lovely and unblemished and showed no evidence of either an accident or a surgeon's scalpel. I had also not seen signs of mental distress, though she was apparently confused about the fact that World War Two had ended sixteen years ago and was expecting to receive news at any time from her husband, who had almost certainly been killed in action.

"Tommy."

And then there was her too quick answer when I asked her if she knew anybody named Sarah. It was as if she had had that answer ready to go in the event somebody was to ask that very question.

"Tommy."

"Huh?"

"I said I was never able to follow up on Mrs. Reissman because she was transferred from JFH into the care of a relative who took her somewhere private to recover."

"A relative; do you know who?"

"I was able to find that out," he said, and flipped ahead a few pages. "It was Vanessa Reissman's aunt; an elderly woman from Chicago named Sarah Goldman. This aunt was the one who made funeral arrangements for the little girl. I only learned of this much after the fact when I ran into Marty Bass— he was the funeral director who handled the burial—down at the Rusty Rooster Bar about a month after the little girl was laid to rest. Bass told me the aunt made all of the arrangements for the little girl's burial and that he never saw the mother at all. The aunt didn't even bother with a Jewish ceremony. There had been no visitation, no funeral service in the funeral home; just a quick burial. Bass told me that the only people in attendance at the graveside service were this aged aunt—whom he described as so old and feeble he thought he might have been able to do a second burial if it had been ten degrees hotter that day—and Abraham Johnson, the wrecker driver who had towed the car."

"Did you ever hear anything more about Vanessa Reissman? No idea of where she went to recover from her injuries? Was there anything at all?" I asked.

"Absolutely nothing," Dennis said. "These were rich people who were only summer residents. Nobody knew them, and they had the kind of money it takes to live private lives. They could hire people from out of the area who would do their bidding and keep their secrets. For all I know, the aunt took Vanessa back to Chicago, or maybe she arranged for a private physician to take care of her in that big house they had way out there in the woods. After my original story ran in the paper, there was nothing to follow up on, and Kessler wouldn't have let me waste time on it anyway."

I sat quietly for a moment and considered what he had just said. With the mother off somewhere recovering from her wounds and her little daughter in the ground, what more was there to write? Wealthy as they were, they weren't famous or noteworthy.

I stood up and thanked Dennis for all of his help and turned to leave when he said, "There is one more little tidbit that I came across. I don't recall who told it to me, and I don't know if it makes any difference, but it was interesting enough for me to jot it down." He held his notebook out to me. I took it and read what he had written down thirteen years ago: the little girl was mute. As I walked out to my truck, I understood why Sarah had not spoken to me when I was with her and what she was trying to communicate to me this morning. She was not able to talk in life, and her handicap persisted in the state in which she now existed. But what I couldn't understand was why Vanessa Reissman had denied knowing a little girl named Sarah when I had asked her this morning if the name meant anything to her. Why deny knowing her daughter?

There were a number of unanswered questions running through my mind, but something was telling me that if I found the answer to this question, all others would be answered.

It was after three o'clock when I left Joshua Falls, and though I wasn't thrilled about seeing the car in which Sarah's short life had ended, I decided to drive to Johnson's Auto Salvage to see if they still had Vanessa Reissman's Ford Pilot. Maybe there was something I could glean from inspecting the wreck. Perhaps seeing the car would help me better grasp what had happened the day Sarah died. Maybe it was just morbid curiosity, though I would like to think it was something more than that. Whatever the reason, I felt compelled to go, but I knew the fawn would be hungry, so I drove home first to feed him even though it would mean doubling back most of the way to Joshua Falls.

Chapter 8

When I arrived at my cabin, I immediately prepared a bottle of the milk replacer and took it to the garage. To my surprise, despite the cast on his leg, the fawn trotted over to me bleating to be fed. I sat down and pushed the nipple into his mouth, and he began his assault on the bottle, head pistoning forward, drool leaking from his muzzle, his tiny flag tail furiously fanning the air. It took only a few minutes of greedy sucking to drain the bottle. I had no doubt he could handle a second, and I had to do some fancy footwork to extract myself from the garage without the fawn slipping out with me. It was obvious that he was improving quickly. If the doe didn't give up and leave the area, I was pretty sure my plan to reunite mother and baby would succeed.

The second bottle disappeared almost as quickly as the first, and I left a contented and somewhat sleepy fawn lying on his quilt in the corner. I went back to my cabin, washed up, and made a sandwich to take on the road. I didn't know how late Johnson's would be open, and I wanted to be sure to arrive with plenty of time to find the Ford if it was still there among the wrecks, rusting away in the weeds of the salvage yard.

It was after five when I pulled into the dirt parking lot of Johnson's Auto Salvage to look for Vanessa Reissman's wrecked Ford Pilot. I maneuvered around several mud-filled potholes and parked in front of a row of tall steel racks overflowing with automobile body parts. Car and truck doors, trunk lids, fenders and hoods, and entire front clips in a muted rainbow of oxidized colors rested on high shelves, and someone had taken a grease pencil and scribbled year and model information on them. One rack was partitioned off with vertical dividers to store windshields upright and keep them from falling over; another strained under the weight of several stripped down engine blocks and half a dozen complete engines. Another of the racks displayed transmissions stacked like cordwood. Everywhere the detritus of salvaged cars and trucks were heaped in piles on the ground and stuffed into wooden bins and rusty barrels. Surrounding it all, a ten-foot high fence made of sheets of corrugated tin hid the mess from view and protected the salvage yard from trespassing scavengers.

I heard a crackling sound coming from behind me and turned to see a large garage with three open overhead doors on the east side of the yard. An old school bus sat in the bay to the far right, and oddly, a ten-foot-tall replica of the Statue of Liberty stood in the center bay where a man in overalls and a welder's mask worked on it amid a shower of sparks and pulsating light.

I noticed two doghouses stationed toward the back of the garage, spaced about thirty feet apart. Two enormous German Shepherds trotted frenetically in an arc at the end of thick chains but, no doubt used to visitors in the yard, did not bark at me.

At the north end of the parking lot were the remains of a burned down ranch style house. It was little more than a pile of charred timbers, broken glass, and melted roofing, but a segment of the front wall remained upright with a door and one window left intact. A single-wide mobile home with a mud-covered front stoop constructed of unpainted lumber had been installed next to the remains of the house. The sign above the door read OFFICE, and a smaller sign on the door itself invited me to walk in.

The bell above the door jingled when I stepped into the salvage yard office and glanced around. An enormous metal desk with chipped gray enamel paint and a drift of paperwork threatening to spill onto the floor stood front and center in the room. On my right sat an old couch covered with a cracked plastic slipcover. A coffee can half filled with sand and bristling with stubbed-out cigarette butts sat on a small end table next to the couch. To my left was a short counter where an electric hot plate sat boiling a pot of coffee dry. The walls of the office were papered with dog-eared and smudge pages stamped INVOICE and RECEIPT. The room smelled of automotive grease and cigar smoke, and the waning daylight filtering in through the windows cast the place in a sickly yellow glow.

I heard a toilet flush, and a moment later, an impossibly large man in dirty overalls opened a door at the far end of the room and squeezed through into the office. He noticed me and walked over. The floor beneath him heaved with every step as he approached. "Help you?" he asked, stopping at the end of the desk.

I opened my mouth to speak and then realized that I hadn't given any thought as to how I would explain my desire to find and examine Vanessa Reissman's Ford. How would I describe my interest in a thirteen-year-old car wreck? Should I pretend to need parts for a similar car that I was repairing? If I went that route, what parts did I need and what if he had what I said I was looking for out there on one of those big metal racks? There would be no need to go out into the yard and find Vanessa Reissman's Pilot.

The big man stood looking at me and rephrased his question. "Is there something I can help you with?" He moved behind the desk and sat down in a sturdy oak chair that rolled on casters. It creaked under his weight as he shifted to get comfortable. I noticed a patch above his left shirt pocket embroidered with the name Abe, and I recalled Dennis Cain reading from his notes earlier that the only people to attend Sarah's burial were the elderly aunt and the wrecker driver, Abraham Johnson. Not being skilled in deception, I decided to come right out and ask if he still had the wrecked Pilot and if I could look at it.

"My name's Tommy Ryan, sir," I said, and stepped forward and offered a handshake. Abe's hand was warm, calloused, and roughly the same size as roasting chicken, yet his handshake was unusually gentle.

"Well, what can I do for you, Tommy?" he said, smiling up at me. "You lookin' to buy some parts, or maybe junk a car? I pay the going rate per pound for salvage, and if its parts you're looking for…well, I got just about anything you may want out there," he said, waving one hand towards the office door. "Biggest salvage yard in Northeastern Wisconsin. Folks come to me from all over because I've got what they're looking for and can't find anywhere else. I even guarantee my parts for a full thirty days from the date of purchase. Whatever you need, I'm sure I've got it."

He delivered this little speech with a beaming sort of pride, and I hated to disappoint him, but I cleared my throat and said, "I'm not here to buy anything." I hesitated for just a moment and then plunged in. "Thirteen years ago, Johnson's Wrecker Service towed a 1947 Ford Pilot that had gone off the road and hit a big pine at the bottom of Eagle Bluff out on Highway 141. A little girl was killed in that accident. I was wondering if that car was still here and if I might take a look at it."

The big man's smile faded, his forehead wrinkled, and his eyes narrowed suspiciously. His chair groaned as he leaned back, unconsciously creating distance between us. I decided I would have to give him some plausible reason for wanting to see the car, and since there was no point in reinventing the wheel, I gave the same explanation I had given to Doctor Rayburn. I told Abe Johnson about finding the faded cross and being curious about the accident that had claimed little Sarah's life.

He listened quietly, and when I finished speaking, he leaned forward again and folded his big, work-hardened hands on top of his desk. He nodded his head slightly but said nothing, and I could see that his eyes had gone moist. When he finally spoke, his words hit me like a wrecking ball. All at once, my legs would no longer support my weight, and I had to take a seat on the plastic covered couch.

"You've seen her," he said. I didn't know how to respond, but it didn't matter because Abe got his answer from the expression on my face. "I've seen her too, out there along the highway in her pretty dress and hat, sitting on the log, sitting where she died."

Chapter 9

I sat on the grimy seat of Abe's old Chevy truck as it bumped along a narrow two-track dirt road that led away from the office into a copse of dense fir and birch trees. Branches scrapped along the side of the truck and slapped at me through my open window as we drove through a quarter-mile of thick forest before emerging from the woods into a vast field of about eighty acres surrounded by what seemed to be an endless stretch of more forest. Abe came to a stop on top of a low rise and let the motor idle. I gazed past the cracks in the windshield at the rusted tops of what looked like thousands of cars and trucks hunching up through the tall spring grass like breaching whales in an emerald green sea.

There didn't appear to be any logic to the distribution of the several thousand junked vehicles. They lay strewn about as if left haphazardly by some giant child after playing with his toys. To the north, I could see the continuation of the two-track road climbing a rise in the topography and meandering past clusters of wrecked cars and trucks. Here and there, I saw derelict farm machinery, rows of old school buses and panel vans, and there was even an old steam shovel lying on its side with one segmented track visible above the tall grass. The panorama before me was pure chaos, and I wondered how Abe found anything, much less knew what he had out there scattered to the horizon.

"That's a lot of old cars and trucks," I said, without looking at Abe.

"Biggest salvage yard in the Northwoods," he said, with an obvious note of pride in his voice. "Hell, we've got just about anything you can think of out there to include Model T Fords, a Stanley or two, even a couple of wrecked airplanes. Our motto is 'You'll find it at Johnson's.' And it's true too. Folks come from as far away as Milwaukee and the Twin Cities to find parts they can't get anywhere else. If I haven't got it on a rack up front, we just head out there," he said, nodding out the windshield, "and find what they're looking for. They may be born in Detroit, but they come here when they die." Abe sat quietly then for a long moment, looking thoughtfully through the windshield.

I looked at Abe and thought about our exchange back in the office. I hadn't known what to say when he confessed that he had also seen Sarah sitting by the side of the road. For a moment, I considered insisting that I was merely curious about the accident, but there seemed to be no point in denying my encounter with the pretty little ghost, so I told him everything, and when I finished, Abe agreed to take me to see Vanessa Reissman's Ford Pilot. It was somewhere out there in that seemingly endless collection of scrap, and I did not doubt that Abe knew precisely where.

The evening sun was lowering in the western sky. Its acute angle stitched a complicated tapestry of shadows across the salvage yard, glinting off glass and chrome here, slipping past dark recesses there. The sun would be below the horizon soon enough, and I wanted to be back home by nightfall. "Maybe we'd better get going, sir," I said.

"Huh?"

"Out to wherever the Pilot is sitting."

"Right," Abe said, and put his hand on the knob of the gearshift, but he didn't put the old truck in gear. "I knew she was Jewish," he said, all at once. "When I placed the cross by the side of the road right after the accident, I knew she was a Jew. I should have put a Star of David there instead. That's always bothered me. Jews don't get crosses, they get the Star of David, but the war had only been over for about two years, and there were a lot of haters around here back then. Hell," he said, "there's plenty around today. A star wouldn't have lasted two days."

"You placed the cross out there?" I asked.

"It didn't seem right, her not having something to mark her passing like others get when they die on the road. You know what I mean. You've seen them crosses stuck into the ground where folks have died in wrecks. That's why I put one there for her." Abe sighed and said, "It just didn't seem right to let her go unremembered." He shook his head disappointingly, "Should have put out a Star of David."

He was quiet again for a moment, and then he said, "I could see her, but I couldn't understand her," I looked at him. His chin was nearly resting on his broad chest; his face was solemn, his voice almost a whisper. He didn't look at me when he spoke.

"Four years ago was when I saw her. I was driving by, just like you were, and there she was, sitting on the big log looking as pretty as a picture in her dress and hat. I pulled over right away because it was getting dark and she was alone. I thought she was lost. I got out and walked over to where she was sitting, and I asked her if she needed help. All she did was point and bounce up and down like she was all excited. She kept putting her hand over her mouth and shaking her head. I asked her name, where she lived, where her mother was, you know…things like that, trying to figure out how I could help her."

Abe filled his lungs with air and swelled his barrel chest even larger, then let out a long shuddering exhale. He began picking at one greasy thumbnail as he spoke.

"I eventually realized she was mute and couldn't speak to me. I got the idea to put her in my truck to drive her over to the Sheriff Happle's office, and when I took hold of her hand and started to lead her toward my truck, she pulled away from me. I knew she was scared and afraid to go with me, but what was I going to do, leave her out there alone with it getting dark?" He shook his head. "I couldn't do that, so I took her hand again and said, 'You have to come with me, honey. You can't stay out here alone.' I started to pull her towards my truck, and that's when things got kind of," he paused as if searching for the right word, "that's when things got all stirred up and excited."

Abe stopped picking at his thumbnail and looked at me. His expression was a mixture of unbelief and fear, and I surmised it was the same one he wore that night, four years ago, when it dawned upon him who he was talking to alongside the highway.

"I was tugging on her arm, telling her it was okay and that I was going to take her to someone who could help her. All at once, I couldn't budge her. I just felt her stop like all of a sudden, she weighed a ton or two. It was like she was anchored to the ground. When I looked at her, there was a sort of hot, white light bleeding right out of her like she was a lampshade over a thousand-watt bulb. It just beamed out of her skin like she'd swallowed the sun or something. But it was her eyes," Abe said, his own going wide as he spoke. "It was her eyes. I have never seen anyone look so confused and sad and angry all at once. She just stood there with that hot light bleeding out of her, shaking like an engine with a broken motor mount."

He went quiet for a moment, and I thought he finished. I was about to prod him into getting me to the Ford before it got any darker, but he took a deep breath and resumed his story.

"The sky was clear when the sun went down, but now…now it was a dark, blackish-purple like it was about to storm and the wind was kicking up a real gale. Leaves were whipping past me, and the trees were rocking like they were going to uproot. I didn't know what to think, and I'll tell you I come all over scared as hell. I dropped her hand and just stood there watching her glow like she was a torch. Then it was like she was a negative, you know, like picture film. She flickered back and forth between light and dark, and she was see-through at times, you know—thin like she was half transparent."

I heard a long inhalation and realized it was me. I had been holding my breath in astonishment as he spoke and didn't know it. I thought he had finished his story, but he said, "She just kept on like that, going bright and then dimming again. It went on for a while and then everything just stopped. The wind blew itself out, the leaves and grass settled down, and the sky took on a soft purple light it gets at twilight. It all just stopped."

As if to illustrate the point, he turned back to staring out across the salvage yard and sat quietly. After a long moment, I asked, "What happened after that?"

"Nothing," he said. "Nothing happened. I was looking around at the trees and sky, the leaves falling back to the ground, I guess I was kind of speechless, and when I looked back at the girl, she was gone." He shrugged his shoulders and said, "Vanished. I never saw her again."

Abe put the truck in gear, and as we rolled forward, he said, "I thank Jehovah that I never saw her that day, you know…the day she died. I didn't get to the scene to pick up the wrecked car until after her body had been taken away. The day I did see her was nine years after the accident, and I didn't realize who she was. I mean, who would? She looked like a lost kid or something. Nine years is a long time, you know. I towed more wrecks than I can remember over those nine years, all up and down that highway. It's a bad stretch in the winter, out there by Eagle Bluff; it ices up all the time. I had forgotten where that Ford Pilot went into the tree, and the cross I put out there had gone missing at some point, I don't even know when. When eventually I figured out who I had been with, I had a case of the nerves for about a week. I kept seeing a shadow flickering about like when someone is welding. I'd catch it out of the corner of my eye, and when I turned my head to see it better, it would be gone. After a while, I didn't see it anymore."

Abe picked up speed, and we drove to the bottom of the hill. "I should have put a star out there," he said, shaking his head.

Abe followed the two-rut through the tall meadow grass past clusters of wrecks and stopped at a sharp curve to the right where the road disappeared around a row of old school buses lined up with their hoods raised on rusted hinges. They reminded me of old soldiers standing at attention for one last inspection.

"The Pilot's about fifty yards down the road on the left," he said. "It sits about thirty yards back, behind a trio of old delivery trucks. You can still see the bakery names painted on the sides, though they're starting to fade into the rust. Look behind the trucks. You can't miss it."

"Aren't you coming, sir?" I asked.

Abe shook his head. "I have to get back and lock the front gate. We close at six. You only have about an hour till sundown, and you'll want to be finished by then. I'll come back to pick you up, but if you finish poking around before then, just follow the road back."

I opened the door and climbed down onto the packed dirt road. We were in a steep valley, and the sun was already dropping behind a rise to the west, pulling deep shadows up between the old junkers. In another twenty minutes, it would be difficult to see much of the interior of Vanessa Reissman's car. "I don't suppose you have a flashlight?" I asked.

Abe leaned over and opened the glove box. He handed me a flashlight. "Batteries may be weak, but it's better than nothing. I'll be back here in an hour unless I find you walking out."

"Thank you," I said, and closed the door.

"Tommy," Abe said, a troubled expression coming over his broad face. "I do have to get back to send my man home and lock up, but that's not the only reason I'm not going with you. The truth is," he hesitated before going on, and I got the distinct impression he was terrified about something, "the truth is I don't like to be around it. I haven't been anywhere near it in years."

I leaned my forearms on the bottom of the open truck window and looked at him. "It's okay," I assured him. "I think I understand."

"No, you don't," he said. "I mean, it's not what you think. It's not the memory of the wreck or who it happened to." Abe's face had a pinched expression as if he tasted something sour. "It's the car. I don't like to be around the car."

"I don't understand, sir, the car?"

Abe looked as if he were about to explain, but then quietly said, "I'll be back in an hour." He put the truck in gear, and I stepped back. He pulled a U-turn using some open space between wrecks and the old truck bumped and rattled back the way it had come. I stood and watched it go until a bend in the road hid it from my sight.

Chapter 10

I found the trio of old bakery trucks and squeezed between two of them, dusting my clothes with chalky paint and rust. When I pushed out on the other side, the roof of the Ford Pilot came into view above the tall meadow grass. I immediately didn't like what I was seeing. Several dozens, perhaps a hundred or more, crows covered every inch of the trunk, roof, and hood of the old Ford like a glossy black pelt. And just like the birds I had seen in the pine where I met Sarah, the ordinarily raucous crows were utterly silent as they jostled for position, hopping past one another, shifting, trading spaces, and then settling in place again. The entire surface of the old car rippled as if it were a living beast, its bunched muscles twitching under a sleek coat so black it almost appeared blue in the evening light.

The eerie sight stopped me in my tracks, and a feeling of dread assailed me.

Leave her—she belongs to the Empty!

I felt the hairs prickle on my skin and a shiver run through my body at the sight of all of those silent crows slithering over Vanessa Reissman's car. It was like hearing the door in my boyhood kitchen slowly creaking open behind me. I was starting to hate crows.

I rubbed down the gooseflesh on my arms and looked up at the soft violet of the earth's shadow in the sky above the eastern horizon. The two things that comfort me most are the evening sky just after sunset and the orange, gold, and crimson of the forest at the peak of its autumnal bloom. I concentrated on the violet sky, and soon I felt foolish standing there wasting daylight.

I moved forward, and after covering several yards, the tall meadow grass abruptly ended, affording me an unobstructed view of the car. The crows protested my sudden appearance by taking to the sky and cawing loudly, as is their habit. They lifted off in unison and moved across the salvage yard like a low hanging storm cloud. I watched them until they disappeared behind a rise in the topography to the west and then turned my attention to the car.

The Pilot was sitting on flat, dry-rotted tires and resting in a circular patch of withered grass as dead and gray as a winter ditch. Nothing green had sprouted for a distance of about twenty feet in all directions. It was as if something toxic had spread out from the car, poisoning the soil. A few cedar saplings closest to the car had succumbed and were nothing more than skeletal remains and a few flat brown needles.

The condition of the car surprised me. Aside from severe damage to the front end, which was visible from where I was standing at the edge of the withered grass, the Ford was remarkably clean and intact. Had Abe not told me that he hadn't been near it in several years, I would have guessed he was maintaining it with regular washings and waxing. Even the crows had spared it the indignation of whitewashing its gleaming black lacquer paint. The Pilot appeared neither blemished by rust nor dulled by successive seasons of Northern Wisconsin weather. In the dull light of evening, its graceful contours and chrome trim looked as if freshly minted.

The car was a right-hand drive. I hadn't expected that. The Pilot was manufactured overseas and imported. This made no real difference, except that Sarah would have been riding in the front left-hand seat rather than the right. The left side of the windshield was little more than jagged shards clinging to the frame, but the glass was still in place on the right side in spite of a starburst of cracks where Vanessa Reissman's head had struck it.

I stepped over to the driver's side door and peered in through the window. The interior was dark, but there was enough light to see that the steering column had been forced up against the dashboard when Vanessa had been thrown forward by the impact with the tree; the same impact that had sent Sarah through the windshield. I have heard that this type of crash usually involves severely broken ribs and extensive internal injuries, often resulting in death, either at the scene or later in the hospital. Vanessa was fortunate to have survived.

I tried the door handle, but the sudden shift of the front of the car rearward upon impact with the big pine had placed considerable pressure on the frame causing the door to bind. I tugged hard and it swung open with a loud groan. I pulled the flashlight Abe loaned me from my pocket and tried the switch. It refused to come on, but a solid slap on the base resulted in a weak yellow beam which I aimed into the front seat.

The interior was littered with shards of glass and an accumulation of detritus that had drifted in through the shattered windshield. I could detect a tangy, metallic odor and the aroma of damp rotting upholstery. I brushed debris from the seat and climbed in behind the severely canted steering wheel and sat there looking through the damaged windshield at the darkening salvage yard. Fortunately, after more than a decade of exposure to the elements, any bloodstains that may have been present had faded, but I did see several strands of blond hair caught between shards of glass that remained in the windshield frame where Sarah had been sitting. I reached up and tugged them free and looked at them for a moment before coiling them around my finger and tucking them into my shirt pocket.

I have read that more than half of all traffic accidents occur within one mile of home. This statistic proved accurate in this case and somehow made the crash seem more tragic. I placed my hands on the steering wheel, feeling the hard, cool plastic, and pictured Vanessa Reissman piloting the big car down the highway, nearly to the turnoff that would have taken her and Sarah to their home, and I wondered what went so tragically wrong.

I don't know how long I sat there wasting time, but I was jolted back to myself by the shrill yapping of a pack of coyotes. Their high-pitched barking resonated through the salvage yard, and once again, the hair on the back of my neck was standing at attention. I noticed that it was nearly full dark, and I felt anxious to finish my examination of the car and get going. If the flashlight gave out altogether, I would be feeling my way back to the dirt road, and that would be dangerous given all the opportunities to trip over things scattered about in the long grass.

I rapped the bottom of the flashlight to get it going again and used the weak beam to look on the front floorboards. I sifted through dried leaves and shattered glass but found nothing remarkable. I turned around and shined the flashlight into the rear seat. Somebody, most likely Abe, had tossed bits of the wreckage onto the back seat. One of the Pilot's headlight buckets lay on the rear bench with a long strip of twisted chrome trim and the front bumper. Likewise, the rear floor, also, was littered with dried leaves and a pile of stuffing that had been pulled from one of the seats and fashioned into what appeared to be a rodent's nest. Two of the Pilot's hubcaps were on the rear floor along with a scattering of acorn and chestnut shells and pellets of animal droppings.

I opened the door and stepped out. Crouching, I used the flashlight to look under the front seat. Something shiny caught my eye, and I reached under, and I fished it out. It was a golden, Victorian Era locket with a woven basket design studded with diamond chips on the cover. It was beautiful, and it reminded me of one my grandmother used to keep in a White Owl cigar box on the top of her dresser. I snapped it open to reveal a photo of a handsome young man standing behind a seated Vanessa Reissman. The young girl standing to her left appeared to be five or six years old and was unquestionably Sarah. I stowed the locket in my pocket and then took it out again. I retrieved the strands of Sarah's hair from my shirt pocket, re-coiled them as best I could, and placed them on top of the photo and snapped the cover. I returned it to my pocket and resumed my search beneath the front seat.

I pulled several handfuls of dead leaves and rotted carpet out and reached in further, but the framework of the seat was digging painfully into the back of my hand. I got up and walked around to the passenger side of the car. Again, the impact with the tree had jammed the door. It came open unwillingly, and not without its own loud protestations, but I was able to pry it open wide enough to allow me to get down on my knees and resume my search beneath the front seat. My fingers closed on something made of cloth, and I pulled my hand out. I was holding a Raggedy Ann doll, soiled and mildewed, but otherwise intact. I stuffed the toy into the waistband of my jeans.

I found nothing more under the seat and moved around to the rear of the car. The spare tire kit was mounted on the outside of the trunk. Beneath it I found the catch to raise the lid. I shined the flashlight inside and was surprised to find it packed with suitcases. I thought about that for a moment. I had assumed Vanessa Reissman and Sarah had been returning to their lake home, maybe from shopping in town or having gone out for a drive, but suitcases in the trunk indicated something else entirely.

In my mind, I brought up the image of the enormous pine and concentrated, trying to see everything I had observed yesterday. It took me a few moments, but it finally came to me. The large, healed-over scar marking where the car had struck the tree had been on the western side of the trunk. I hadn't realized this, nor would I have, given the unusual circumstances of finding a little girl sitting all alone by the side of the road, but I could see it clearly now. The only way the tree would have been struck on the west side would have been if the car had been traveling to the east, away from the direction of their home. Vanessa and Sarah were not nearly home; they had just left.

Feeling a bit like a burglar, I opened the largest of the cases. It was clear from the contents that it belonged to Vanessa rather than Sarah. On top of the folded clothes was an envelope containing documents of some sort. I am not sure why, but I tucked the envelope into my back pocket and resumed my search of the trunk. Aside from the suitcases, I found nothing significant.

I considered the suitcases, and I resolved to come back to the Pilot to retrieve them and return them to Vanessa, but I had no desire to carry them out with me now. I took the Raggedy Ann from my waistband and placed it in the suitcase, then closed it. I reached up to give the trunk lid a good slam, but then pulled my hand away quickly. The metal was unnaturally cold. My fingers and the palm of my hand burned as if I had touched a block of dry ice. In the low glow of the flashlight, my breath was a vapor curling up toward the open lid of the car's trunk. I reached up again and quickly slammed the trunk lid and then gave the car a once-over with the beam of my flashlight. A face was looking out at me through the rear window.

I nearly fell on my backside. I dropped the flashlight, and the beam winked out. I was thrust into darkness, complete except for a dim glow very low on the western horizon. Bitter cold air assaulted my exposed skin, and I began to shiver, though not entirely from the cold. Standing there alone, I heard the distinct sound of the headlight bucket falling off the back seat onto the floorboard and clanging into the hubcaps.

A raccoon! Maybe a raccoon climbed into the car while I was searching the trunk. That's what it is. A raccoon climbed in, and that's what I'll see when can get the flashlight working again. Just reach down and pick it up and take a look.

I don't know how I convinced my body to respond to my mental commands, but I managed to find the flashlight next to my right foot where it had landed. Everywhere around me was utter stillness, except for the sounds coming from within the Pilot. Something in there was moving. I could hear the dried leaves on the floor rustling and the clatter of metal upon metal.

I tried the flashlight again, but nothing happened. Perhaps the batteries had finally given out, or maybe the bulb had broken when I dropped it. I rapped it on the bottom several times and was about to give up when again I was rewarded with a weak yellow glow which I immediately trained upon the rear window of the Pilot. For a moment, the light reflected off the glass, and I could see nothing. I adjusted the angle of the beam and gasped audibly. It was not a raccoon.

One grief-stricken eye in a ghastly, disfigured face peered out from a swaddle of blood-soaked bandages. Most of the lower jaw and mouth were missing, and the pulpy mess that remained moved in a hideous parody of speech, clicking and stuttering up and down on its broken hinge. The face was caked in mud and portions of exposed skin were charred black with burns. Below the ruined face I could see a blood-soaked olive-colored T-shirt.

I couldn't move. Fright had robbed me of all motor skills, and yet my senses seemed to be working at a heightened level. I suppose that is what happens when one suddenly finds one's self wholly immobilized by fear. Perhaps in moments of abject terror, the mind, often a cruel actor, shifts resources to the senses of sight and hearing to make up in some small way for depriving us of our muscular control. All the better, I suppose, to hear our hearts pounding in our chests and to see our doom approaching.

The flashlight winked out again. I repeatedly rapped the base of the light, trying to coax a beam from the failing batteries, but was rewarded with nothing. As I frantically tried to get the flashlight working again, I prayed the impact with the tree had jammed the rear doors more solidly than it had the front. I cannot tell you with any certainty what I would have done had the phantasm found its way out of the car to shamble through the dark in my direction, but I am confident I would not have come out of the experience unscathed. A blind flight across the cluttered salvage yard would have been perilous.

My dread was working against me. I could accomplish nothing in my mental state. For the second time since finding the Pilot, I willed myself to calm down and made sure the flashlight was switched on. I gave the bottom one last solid slap, and thin light once again fell upon the rear window of Vanessa Reissman's car. In the dim glow, I watched as the inside of the Pilot's rear window covered over with frost, spreading like crystal feathers from the outside edges toward the center. Just before the beam of my flashlight winked out for good, I saw a fingertip pressed against the glass from the inside. It etched two words in the ice:

HELP THEM

Chapter 11

The trip back to the dirt road would have been dangerous had Abe not arrived when he did and honked his horn and directed his old truck's headlamps between the bakery trucks. It was still slow going, but I walked toward the glare feeling carefully for anything that might trip me and cause me to fall and injure myself.

I told Abe about the suitcases on the way back to the salvage yard office. He knew about them but hadn't known what to do with them since nobody had ever come to claim them and he had had no idea where to send them. He had opted to just leave them undisturbed in the trunk.

Abe asked no questions, and I offered no narrative, but I recalled what he had said to me about not liking to go near the car and now understood why. We may talk about it one day, but it could wait.

When we arrived back at the office, Abe went to open the gate for me. I stopped before driving out onto the road and rolled down the window to thank him. He walked over and placed his hands on the bottom edge of my open window and said, "I took a look at the car after bringing it here. I was curious about something I noticed at the accident scene, and I just wanted to check it out for myself."

I didn't respond, and he continued. "There were no skid marks on the road. No brake marks, I mean. It was like the car just drove off the road; like she didn't hit the brakes at all."

That struck me as odd. It's a natural reaction for any driver to go for the brakes, even if it's the wrong thing to do under the circumstances of the moment.

Abe continued, "I looked under the hood thinking maybe the throttle linkage was jammed up and maybe the gas pedal stuck or something." He hesitated a moment before saying, "It was fine. That Ford was almost new back then, and it was in great shape. I never did find a mechanical reason for why she went off the road and piled into that big pine."

I nodded and said goodnight, and Abe responded by slapping my door twice as he turned to walk over to the gate. I don't remember the trip home. I was too deep in thought.

Chapter 12

I fed the fawn and spent several minutes stroking its silky, spotted coat and admiring its dark, liquid eyes. Doctor Rayburn had said I had about 72 hours to care for the fawn before the mother would abandon it and move on. It had only been about 36 hours, so if the good doctor was right, she was likely still keeping close, but I must admit there was a part of me that hoped she would abandon the little guy. I had already decided that if the doe moved on, I'd raise him. A pet deer would make a delightful companion. But deep down I knew where he belonged, and I was determined to see him back with his mother and free.

I had no desire to even think about the events of the day until I had a shower and something to eat. Only after emptying my water heater of every drop and wolfing down a heaping plate of scrambled eggs and fried ham and potatoes did I sit down at my kitchen table to look at the two items I had brought home with me.

I picked up the locket and re-examined the photo inside, being careful not to lose the strands of Sarah's hair. I used a kitchen knife to lift the little photo from its resting place and turned it over. Written in a delicate script was:

The loves of my life,
Robert and Sarah.
April 1944.

I did the math. If Sarah had been about eight years old when she died, she would have been four or five years old, at the most, at the time the picture had been taken. I turned the photo back over and held it close to a small lamp I keep on the table. With the aid of good lighting, the slightly grainy black and white photo was much easier to see than it had been in the salvage yard where I had only the dim light of the flashlight. I looked carefully at the happy family pictured there. Vanessa was wearing a pretty floor-length, high-collared dress. She was seated and turned slightly to her left. Sarah was wearing a formal dress with lace at the collar and sleeves and standing on her mother's left side. Standing behind them both, Robert Reissman looked serious and handsome in his Class A US Army uniform.

HELP THEM

A cold chill ran down my spine as it became clear whom I had encountered in the salvage yard earlier; the very man Vanessa Reissman was faithfully waiting for; a husband who was never coming home.

I replaced the photo and the strands of Sarah's hair and snapped the cover on the locket. I hung it over the napkin holder in the center of my table and turned my attention to the manila envelope. It was bigger than a standard envelope and closed with a string tie, which was missing. I blew into it and tipped its contents onto the table. There were two documents: a Western Union telegram and an official looking envelope containing a letter.

I picked up the telegram and examined it. Several thin strips of white paper typed with uppercase letters and no punctuation were glued to its surface. It read:

WESTERN UNION

31 GOVT
WASHINGTON DC 845PM 5-16-45
VANESSA REISSMAN
THE SECRETARY OF WAR WISHES ME TO EXPRESS HIS DEEPEST REGRET THAT YOUR HUSBAND CAPTAIN ROBERT V REISSMAN HAS BEEN DECLARED MISSING IN ACTION IN LUZON PHILIPPINES IF FURTHER DETAILS OR OTHER INFORMATION ARE RECEIVED YOU WILL BE PROMPTLY NOTIFIED
UL10 THE ADJUTANT GENERAL

I fingered the corner of the sixteen-year-old telegram contemplatively. Vanessa had spoken proudly of her husband serving in the Pacific Theater, but at no time did she mention, or even intimate, that he had been declared missing in action.

I suppose she may have deemed that information too personal to share with a perfect stranger, or maybe she withheld it out of a concern for her safety; better to have a strange man believe there was a war hero husband to defend her honor. But it was clear from the statements she made that she was living with the belief that the war in the Pacific was still going on in 1961, but why?

I set the telegram aside and picked up the envelope. It was from the War Department in Washington. It was dated June 15, 1948, and postmarked June 29, 1948—the very day of the accident that injured Vanessa and took the life of her daughter.

War Department
The Adjutant General's Office
Washington D.C.

June 15, 1948
Mrs. Vanessa Reissman
17 Halls Road
Alibi Township, Wisconsin

Dear Mrs. Reissman,

It is with my most profound regret that I must notify you that your husband, Captain Robert V. Reissman, missing in action since May 8, 1945, upon identifying his remains, has been confirmed to have died on that date in Luzon, Philippines. There is little I can write to assuage your sorrow, but I want you to know that I have been informed of Captain Reissman's service in the army. From the first day of your husband's service, he worked diligently to establish an exemplary record, and his superior officers recognized his untiring efforts. The reputation achieved by your husband is a fine one, and I hope this knowledge affords you pride and comfort during your time of sorrow. I extend my heartfelt sympathy to you and other members of your family.

Very sincerely,
H.H. Thompson
General, U. S. Army
Commanding General, Army of the Pacific

I read the letter twice and then laid it on the table and picked up the telegram again. The news that her husband was missing in action had arrived nearly three years before the letter declaring his death. I tried to imagine how Vanessa would have felt during those intervening years, not knowing if her husband was dead or alive. I could easily imagine her agonizing for three long years, thinking through every possible scenario: injury, amnesia, capture, anything that would leave him alive to eventually return to her and their daughter. I do not doubt that the day the telegram arrived declaring her husband MIA had been the day she began her long and anxious vigil, praying night and day for his safe return.

I slipped the telegram and letter back into the envelope and recalled how Vanessa had spoken of the war in the present tense and had gone so far as to admonish me to keep up to date about the war, as if I could just read about it in the daily news.

HELP THEM

The words scratched on frosty glass came back to me without prompting, and I shuddered at the memory of the ravaged face looking at me through the rear window of Vanessa Reissman's Ford. I shook off the image and hoped I could keep it away for the rest of the night. When I go back to the salvage yard to retrieve the suitcases, I would do it during broad daylight so there would be no need for a flashlight.

"Suitcases," I said out loud, and chewed the inside of my lip, which I was prone to do when deep in thought. It's my "tell." Those packed suitcases were significant, but how? I thought and chewed for a minute or two before it came to me. According to the postmark, the letter from the War Department had arrived on June 29, 1948. The trunk of the Pilot was packed with suitcases. Important documents were in the car. The scar on the big pine was on the west side of the old tree.

They were leaving. No, that was not accurate; they were fleeing. When the letter with the news of Robert's death had come, Vanessa must have lost her desire to stay at Summer Rest. Its memories, most of them undoubtedly created with her husband, almost certainly no longer comforted her and may have had the opposite effect. Very likely overwrought and crying and in an incredibly emotional state, Vanessa had packed their belongings into the Pilot, and she and Sarah fled Summer Rest, most likely to go back to family in Chicago.

I could almost see it in my mind; Vanessa is sobbing, beside herself with grief, dabbing a handkerchief to her red-rimmed and puffy eyes, perhaps in her anguish, driving too aggressively, maybe running off the road and overcorrecting as she attempted to get the big car back on course. Maybe, in her emotional state, she pressed down on the gas pedal instead of the brake, and the tree looming before her was more than a match for her car.

The yapping of coyotes near my cabin interrupted my thoughts, and I decided to get some air. I got an RC from the fridge and went out to take a peek at the fawn. I walked over to the garage and looked in on him over the open half-door and found him asleep on his quilt. I glanced around for the doe; hopeful she didn't have a keen sense of time passing. Doctor Rayburn's 72-hour clock was ticking, and though I thought it best to keep the fawn a while longer to make sure his leg was going to be okay; I knew the best place for him was with his mother. I didn't want her to abandon him.

I was on my way back to my cabin when the mistake in my thinking revealed itself. I was wrong about Vanessa believing the war was still raging in 1961. She didn't think that all. She believed it was 1945. To Vanessa, the war was a current event. Mr. Murrow was reporting news of America's progress against the enemy. Newspapers were running stories heralding victories and decrying losses in the epic struggle. Somehow, Vanessa Reissman was stuck in 1945 and convinced that her beloved husband was merely missing in action and not dead. After sixteen years, she was still keeping her vigil.

Was it the injuries she had received in the accident that had caused her delusion? I thought it very likely. Not only had she sustained severe injuries to her chest and head, but upon waking, she would have been informed of the death of her little girl and would also have been reminded of the death of her husband. After three long years of anxiety taking a toll on her nerves, this tragic news was likely just too much to bear. I suspected Vanessa was dealing with her grief by clinging to a time when her husband was still alive, and at the same time, denying the daughter she had lost; the daughter she almost certainly felt responsible for killing.

It was almost too much to believe, and I knew I'd be thinking it through all night long, fine-tuning my theory instead of sleeping, but it did explain why Vanessa denied knowing her own daughter and perhaps why Sarah seemed unwilling or unable to leave the place where she had died. The most important person in her young life was refusing to recognize her passing or honor her memory. Perhaps with that kind of unresolved emotion, Sarah could do nothing more than haunt that stretch of highway until her mother came to say a proper goodbye and reestablish a severed connection.

Chapter 13

I am a morning person by nature, waking early, anxious to get moving and experience the offerings of a new day. I rarely hear my old wind-up alarm clock. I wake, instead, to the gentle chime of my internal clock, a few minutes before the one on my nightstand sounds off. However, this morning my internal clock overslept, and I woke feeling thickheaded and groggy at the insistence of my Westclox Baby Ben.

I had lain awake until the wee hours of the morning thinking over everything I had learned the day before and resisting the urge to look into the dark corners of my bedroom for uninvited guests. Despite the hours spent thinking and not sleeping, I still had no concrete idea what it was that Sarah wanted from me. What did her silent yet urgent beseeching mean? What help could I offer a spirit incapable of communicating with me other than by means of pantomime?

While I still did not have an answer to this question, not everything was a mystery. I didn't know what had caused Vanessa's Ford to run off the road that day, but I suspected the reason had come in the envelope from Washington. After three long years of living with the hope that her husband would be found alive, Vanessa had received the worst possible news. I could only imagine how painful that news must have been and how much torment it had caused her not being able to touch him one last time or to express her love or to say goodbye.

There it was again. It was becoming a recurring theme. Vanessa had been cheated out of the opportunity to say goodbye to her husband and Sarah may have had the same experience with her mother. By contrast, my experience with my father's death had been entirely different. I had had ample time to say goodbye and to internalize the fact that he was leaving my mother and me. In the end, there had been a body to bury and an opportunity to mark a point in time where I would move beyond the past with my father and steel myself for a future without him. I have heard that the proper psychological term for this is "closure." I had it, Vanessa and Sarah did not.

Vanessa Reissman had been removed from the hospital in Joshua Falls to recuperate in some private location and had, at some point, come back to Summer Rest. Lying in bed, listening to the spring peepers singing from the stream at the bottom of the slope behind my cabin, I considered the possibility that when she came back to Summer Rest, she did so with no memory of Sarah and the fatal accident that killed her daughter. Perhaps it was a self-defense mechanism designed to spare her from the accompanying guilt. Maybe it was the result of the head trauma she had suffered in the accident. Either way, the result was the same.

It also seemed apparent that Vanessa came back to a time before the arrival of the letter from the War Department declaring her husband killed in action; she came back to a time when Robert was only missing in action, inevitably to be found among the wounded on a hospital ship or held captive in a prisoner of war camp. She came back to a meaningful time when she still had hope that he would one day walk through the door and they would go on with their lives.

The more I thought about it, the more it fit. A combination of profound guilt and unyielding hope was very likely fueling her delusion. I needed to challenge that delusion and force her to deal with the issues she was suppressing. I needed her to remember her daughter. I needed Vanessa to reach out to her and set her free. Perhaps in doing so, Vanessa would also free herself.

Chapter 14

I looked outside at a day cloaked in dense fog. It lay like a gauzy veil across my yard, revealing only ghostly images of the tops of the tall firs and maples at the edge of my lawn. I put on a pot of coffee, and while it perked on the stove, I went out to feed the fawn. As I made my way to the garage, two bottles of milk replacer in hand, I admired the morning. The moist air held the aroma of humus-rich soil and pine resin. The sun would be out later to burn off the fog, but until then, everything was dripping and fresh.

A pair of thrush called from deep in the woods. Their complicated warble had both a note of sadness and inquisitiveness, as if one lost lover were calling out to another. I enjoyed the back and forth between the pair, but soon they were competing with the shrill whistle of a male cardinal advertising for a mate from a perch high in the tip of a century old hemlock. Add in the odd assorted chickadee calling out "Marco Polo" and the frantic screeching of several jays and "nature's glee club," as my mother used to call it, was in rare voice.

When I reached the garage and looked in over the half-door, the fawn was standing on all fours putting weight on his injured leg. I slipped in, and he trotted over to me eager for his breakfast. I sat on an overturned five-gallon bucket and smiled as, once again, the little flag of his tail whipped and spun as he slurped his first bottle in record time. I had just offered up the second when a voice startled me.

"He's looking good, Tommy. I think you've done it."

"Good morning, sir," I said.

Doctor Rayburn was leaning on both forearms watching me from the half-door.

He grinned around the pipe in his mouth and said, "He's putting weight on it. That's the best sign you could hope for."

He slipped the latch and stepped in, squatted next to the fawn, and while the little guy was occupied with breakfast, examined his leg and the cast he had fashioned. He exhaled around the stem of his unlit pipe and grinned up at me. "This looks perfect. There's no reason to think it won't just fall away in time." He stood up and slipped both hands in his pants pockets and watched the fawn finish the bottle.

"He's got a good appetite," I said. "He takes two bottles every time I feed him, and he's not shy about it either. Comes right over and gets down to it."

"I can see that," Doctor Rayburn said. "I'd say your rescue mission is a success."

The fawn was sucking air now, and I pulled the nipple from his mouth. His little tongue flicked in and out of his muzzle several times, and then he backed up, kicking his rear legs into the air before shooting forward and skipping across the floor of the garage. He reached the far wall and turned and skipped back, obviously feeling playful on a full stomach. Doctor Rayburn and I had a good laugh at this and hurried out the door before the fawn could slip out with us.

124

"The way he's prancing around in there," the doctor said, "I'd say the fracture isn't going to be much of a problem."

"I'm happy about that, sir," I said, "but I'm a bit concerned about the doe." We stopped halfway to my cabin and faced each other. "I haven't seen her since you pointed her out to me yesterday. She could just be staying back in the woods, but I'd feel a whole lot better if I saw her."

Doctor Rayburn took a wooden match from his pocket and ran it down the zipper of his jacket. I waited while he lit his pipe, and then we continued walking to my cabin and stepped into the kitchen. I poured coffee in two mugs, and we sat at my table. Doctor Rayburn tried a few puffs, then re-lit his pipe and puffed on it thoughtfully.

"I wouldn't be too concerned about not seeing the doe. She's likely still out there keeping close; probably shows up five minutes after your gone and you just don't know it," he said.

I took a sip from my mug and said, "I hope so. I'd like to see them reunited, but what do I do with him if his mother has given up and moved on? I mean…I could raise him and see to it he survives to adulthood and then release him, but what happens come November of next year? By then, he'll have antlers. He may walk right up to a hunter."

Doctor Rayburn said nothing and examined the burnt tobacco in the bowl of his pipe for a moment. I got up and took an ashtray from my cupboard and placed it in front of him. "Thank you, Son," he said, and removed a pipe nail from his shirt pocket and set about digging out the ash and dottle from the chamber. He blew through the stem a few times, reexamined the bowl, and slipped the pipe into his shirt pocket.

"Well," he said, "let's not get the applecart before the horse. There's no reason to suspect that little fella's mom is not out there. If she is, I recommend getting them back together as soon as possible."

I took a sip from my mug and said, "I'd like to do it tomorrow."

"I think that sounds right," Doctor Rayburn said. "Have you given any thought about how to do it? How are you going to make sure he finds her? You can't just release him and hope they find each other. You have to get them together at the time of the release."

I leaned back and stretched my legs beneath the table and clasped my hands behind my head to stare at the ceiling. I do my best thinking that way. After a few moments, I said, "I can't hang around here all day just waiting to see if the doe shows up, but I'd like to know if she does. If I can be sure she's still here, I'd figure out a way to get them together."

Doctor Rayburn assumed the same thinking posture. After a moment, he sat up and snapped his fingers. "Come with me out to my truck," he said, getting to his feet. I followed him outside and over to where he had parked.

"I've got a bag of barn lime in here. I use it in my horse stalls. You say you're going to be gone today?"

I nodded. "Yes, sir. I've got some errands to run that'll take me most of the day."

He slid the heavy bag of barn lime out of the truck and handed it to me. "Take this lime and spread it on the driveway in front of your garage. Anything that walks over it will leave clear tracks. I wager you'll see deer tracks in it when you get home. If they go up close to your garage by that half-door you leave open, you'll know the doe is paying her little buck visits when you're not around."

"That's a great idea, sir," I said. "At least I'll know for sure, and I can figure out my next step. If she's still around, I'll get him back to her."

Doctor Rayburn slammed the tailgate of his truck and said, "Good luck with the lime. I hope it works. If I don't see you before you release the fawn, tell me all about it when next you see me."

"Yes, sir," I said, and started toward the garage. Then I recalled the message the librarian had given to me for Doctor Rayburn. I set the heavy bag of lime down and trotted over to his truck. Doctor Rayburn was sitting inside examining some documents on a clipboard. I knocked on the window, and he rolled it down. The sweet aroma of cherry pipe tobacco drifted out.

"I forgot to give you a message," I said.

"What's that?"

"Edna Rollins says she has some issues of *Wild West Weekly* dating back to 1908 for you to read."

With almost child-like glee, the doctor clapped his hands together and said, "Oh boy! That's terrific!"

"You must really like reading that *Wild West* stuff, huh?"

"Tommy," he said, his eyes positively glowing, "I think I was born a century out of date. If I could go back in time, I'd be a wrangling fool on some big ranch in Colorado. Instead, here I am trying to wrangle a living out of doctoring livestock for farmers who sometimes pay me with their wives' fried chicken and an offer of kittens for my barn."

I laughed and said, "Yes, sir. I'll tell Mrs. Rollins you'll be by to take a gander at them."

"You do that," he said, and drove out of my driveway.

I spread the lime as Doctor Rayburn had instructed and then scanned the edge of the forest for a few minutes, hoping to see the doe. She was nowhere in sight, and I went into my cabin, had a quick breakfast, and then took the envelope with the telegram and the letter from the War Department and the locket and headed out to my truck.

Chapter 15

My first stop was the library. I arrived about fifteen minutes before it opened and had to wait, but it gave me some time to think about how to get what I had come for. I wasn't certain how cooperative Mrs. Rollins would be about letting me borrow the June 30, 1948 copy of the *Falls Herald*, after all, she told me to tell Doctor Rayburn that he was welcome to read the old issues of *Wild West Weekly*, but he would have to read them in the library. Would she guard old issues of the local newspaper as stringently? I didn't know, but I intended to find out.

When I saw the assistant librarian, Janet, appear in the windows of the massive front doors of the library, I got out of my truck and walked across the street and up the broad concrete steps. She saw me coming and unlocked the doors and pushed one open as I approached. I was the first customer in the building and was able to see Edna Rollins immediately. I don't know why, but I was nervous about asking my favor. Maybe it was that I still saw librarians much as I saw teachers when I was a boy—stern authoritarians with wooden rulers poised to smack noisy children on their knuckles. More likely it was that I was about to tell another lie to get what I wanted, but the knuckle thing was a possibility too.

Mrs. Rollins greeted me warmly, and I told her that I had delivered her message to the good doctor and that he was sure to be in one day soon. She thanked me and asked me if that was all I stopped in for.

"No, ma'am," I said, and was surprised to feel my ears burning as if they were severely sunburned. I was sure they were glowing like Rudolph's famed nose.

"Well, what can I do for you?" she asked.

"Ma'am," I nearly stammered, "I'd like to check out that copy of the *Falls Herald* you helped me find yesterday."

"Certainly," she said, without hesitation, and I was surprised when she stepped into her office and came back with it. I was out the door in twenty minutes and on my way to Johnson's Salvage Yard, and I owed it all to Carl O. Olson, an employee of National Cash Register and the inventor of a new process called "Microfiche."

Mrs. Rollins was only too happy to give me the newspaper because, due to my interest in it yesterday, she had selected it to be the very first publication to be transferred to microfilm, a process of transferring print to a transparent film and storing the printed information in miniaturized form which could then be read by a special microfiche reader that magnifies the image for reading.

I was amazed when she showed me the finished product, a small roll of plastic film, much like camera film, only with images of the individual pages of the newspaper. I could hardly believe that such advanced technology would find its way to the Northwoods of Wisconsin. Mrs. Rollins explained that through a special state grant, the library had been able to purchase the equipment with which they would eventually transfer all periodicals to microfilm, thereby eliminating the need to store the physical copies, saving the library, as she put it: "scads of room." Mrs. Rollins graciously presented me with the newspaper to keep "as it would no longer be necessary to retain it."

I left the library with my mind spinning as I thought of the marvelous time in which I was living: spaceships orbiting the earth and newspapers shrunk down small enough to fit into a tiny canister you can hold in the palm of your hand. What would be next, cars that run on electricity and phones without wires? Jules Vern was probably smiling down upon us.

I arrived at Johnson's a little after ten o'clock and found Abe at his desk. I told him I wanted to head out back to get the suitcases which I intended to deliver to Vanessa Reissman later in the day. Abe said nothing. He quietly stood and walked over to a closet door and pulled it open. Inside were the suitcases.

"You reminded me of them yesterday, so I went out to the Pilot early this morning. I figured you'd come by for them."

"Did you see anything…you know, out of the ordinary when you went out there?" I asked wondering if Abe had, perchance, encountered Robert Reissman.

"You mean the crows?" He asked, and before I could say anything, he added, "There's always crows around that old car. They showed up about a week after I dropped it there and they've been hanging around ever since."

"What do you make of that?" I asked.

Abe sat back down and folded his hands on top of his desk. "My grandparents on my father's side came here from Poland. My grandmother was a deeply religious woman but also very superstitious. She believed in the ancient folklore of the old country and spoke of it all the time when I was a boy. I remember her telling me that every crow is a minion of evil. She told me crows are drawn to the places where restless spirits linger in despair. She said, sometimes when someone dies unexpectedly, their soul feels a powerful sense of having some important business left undone. The frustration they feel over, what she called a 'life interrupted,' can bind a spirit to a particular place and keep them from moving on. She said it's like a profoundly depressed person who can't drag themselves out of bed and take care of life. According to the old legends, the devil is attracted to the despair they feel, and he keeps tabs on these 'empty souls' through his minions, waiting for the right moment to capture them and bind them in hell."

Leave her. She belongs to the Empty.

The thought hit me like a punch from a prizefighter, and I flinched. Abe saw it and asked me if I was alright. I said I was and gathered up the suitcases and took them out to my truck and placed them in the box. Abe followed me outside, and I thanked him again for his help. We shook hands, and he said, "What are you going to do now?"

It was a good question. I knew my next step was to go back to Summer Rest and have another conversation with Vanessa Reissman. I had learned a lot since speaking with her yesterday, and what Abe had said about crows, lingering spirits, and unfinished business was like seed sown in fertile soil. I was starting to understand what Sarah wanted me to do for her. I decided to make a quick stop home to give the fawn a bottle and give it all some more thought on the way.

When I arrived at my cabin, I went immediately inside and mixed up two bottles of milk replacer. I planned on driving over to speak with Vanessa, and I didn't know how long I would be gone. I didn't want a hungry fawn waiting for me.

I stepped off my stoop and started toward my garage and saw the barn lime standing out white against the pink crushed granite driveway gravel. I had forgotten about my little experiment to see if the doe was keeping tabs on her baby. I felt my spirit lift when, from a distance, I saw tracks in the powdery lime. It appeared that she had come out from the cover of the woods and walked right up to the garage. I could see tracks all over the limed area, right up to the half-door.

As I closed the distance, disappointment and fear knocked my soaring spirit out of the sky like a well-placed shotgun blast. The tracks were not from the doe at all. They were canine. They were the tracks of a pack of coyotes. Their paw prints were easily discernable in the white dust and on the boards of the half-door where they had leaped up. I felt my heart leap into my throat. I dropped the two bottles as I bolted up to the door and looked in, totally unprepared for what I would find.

The fawn lay in the middle of the floor, big eyes looking in my direction, happy to see me looking in on him. I exhaled the breath I hadn't realized I had been holding and walked over to retrieve the two bottles of milk replacer. As the fawn fed, I realized that my chances of reuniting him with his mother were getting slimmer by the hour. I also decided that, from now on, I would keep the top half of the door closed.

Chapter 16

Thanks to Abe's grandmother, I felt I had a pretty good idea of what it was Sarah needed from me, and on the drive to Summer Rest, I tried to figure out just what I would say to Vanessa Reissman. If, as I suspected, she was living a delusional life wherein it was 1945, she believed that she had no child and was patiently awaiting the return of a husband serving in in the Philippines, I had to proceed cautiously. After all, I am by no means a psychiatrist, nor any kind of mental health professional, and I was traversing unexplored territory without as much as a compass.

I made the turn north onto Halls Road, and within a few minutes, I turned into the same narrow lane I had used yesterday when I first visited Summer Rest. As low hanging branches slapped my windshield, I wished I had looked further for the main driveway. If I ever had to come here again, I would do so.

I parked where I had the day before and got out. I stepped over to the box of my truck and stowed the locket, the envelope with the telegram, the letter from Washington, and the copy of the *Falls Herald* Edna Rollins had given to me in the same large suitcase where I had placed the rag doll I found yesterday while searching Vanessa Reissman's

Pilot. I tucked two cases below my arms and took two more by their handles and began walking toward the house.

My trip across the lawn was cumbersome, and it took a few minutes. The sun had come out, and I expected to see Vanessa contentedly going about her gardening, but she was nowhere in sight, and I wondered if I had come on a day when she was away, perhaps shopping.

I made my way up onto the big porch and set the suitcases down near the wicker furniture where we had talked yesterday. I knocked on the door, sure somebody, perhaps a servant, would be home. I wasn't sure what I would do if Vanessa were away. Leaving the suitcases without an explanation seemed cruel, although, and I am ashamed to admit this, that is exactly what I was thinking about doing. I knocked again.

I was about to give up and carry everything back to my truck when I caught sight through the window of a figure of a woman moving toward the door. She appeared hazy through the lace curtains, and when the door opened, I was pleased to see Vanessa, who was dressed in the same gardening togs she had worn yesterday.

"Well, Mr. Ryan," she said, smiling. "How pleasant it is to see you again."

"Thank you, ma'am," I said. "It is nice to see you too."

"What brings you back to Summer Rest so soon after our last visit?" she asked, and I noticed she opened the door only far enough to offer a narrow view of herself, not as wide as one might when they intended to welcome a guest across the threshold. Again, I wondered if she was alone in the big house and whether or not she had any servants to keep her company, but I didn't go there this time. She didn't seem to like the question when I asked it yesterday.

"Well, ma'am," I said, "I wonder if we might talk again," I didn't want her to think I was trying to invite myself inside, so I quickly added, "out here on the porch where we visited before?"

"I suppose so," she said and slipped cat burglar-like through the narrow gap in the door, closing it behind her. We walked over to the wicker and took the same seats we occupied the day before, only this time, four suitcases were sitting on the floor before the spindled railing. "What is it you would like to talk about? If you've come back for a second time today to ask for a job," she said, "I'm afraid I am fully staffed."

Second time today? I let that go, and said, "No, ma'am, that's not it." She was looking suspiciously at the suitcases, and it occurred to me that she might suppose I was looking for a place to stay. "Mrs. Reissman," I began, "I've come to tell you of an extraordinary experience I had near your home two days ago, and I think you can help me more fully understand it."

"Is that so?"

"Yes, ma'am," I said, and the expression that came over her face betrayed a curiosity, if not outright suspicion. She adjusted her posture to indicate that I had her full attention. I said, "I was on my way home from work and had a chance meeting with a beautiful little girl whom I found sitting alone by the side of the road. She could not speak, but she made it known to me that her name is Sarah and she is eight years old."

I checked for a reaction to my words, but Vanessa merely looked at me without changing her expression in the least. She remained ramrod straight in her chair with her hands folded primly upon her lap, and I thought, *The same posture Sarah used when I was with her.* I went on, "Sarah led me into the woods and to the shore of your lake." I pointed to the shore on the far side of the lake and said, "Just there, where you see the large tree standing above the others."

I saw Vanessa's eyes flick to the horizon and then settle back on my face, and I noticed that she was now clasping her hands so tightly her knuckles were going white. I said, "Sarah pointed out this house, and she seemed quite sad as we stood together looking across at your home. Though she didn't say so in words, it was clear to me that she believed this was her home too."

Vanessa said nothing. She just sat there looking at me, and I remembered an old sales tactic I had learned from my Uncle Pete, who was very likely the best used car salesman in all of Wisconsin: *the first one to speak loses.*

An uncomfortably long moment passed between us, and I was just about to break Uncle Pete's rule when Vanessa said, "That's quite a fanciful tale, Mr. Ryan, but I really have no time to listen to this."

She started to stand, and I reached out and gently placed a restraining hand upon her arm. *Time to go for broke*, I thought, and said. "Mrs. Reissman, I know this may be difficult to hear, but I believe that you had a daughter and the little girl I encountered is her spirit." Vanessa sat back down, and a pained expression came over her face. "Did you have a daughter named Sarah who died thirteen years ago in a car accident?" I asked.

I found myself holding my breath in anticipation of what would come next. Considering this woman's state of mind and all she had been through, she may very well stand up and order me to leave her property and never speak with me again. On the other hand, if Vanessa's earlier denial of her daughter was the result of overwhelming guilt brought about by the accident, she may break down, become overwrought, and terminate our conversation by demanding that I leave her property. There was also the possibility that she would remain stoic and continue her denial and ask me to leave her property. Regardless, I thought being tossed off her estate was a given.

Vanessa made no denial, so I quickly said, "I have something to show you." I pulled Sarah's suitcase onto the coffee table between us and opened it so that Vanessa could see its contents. I remained quiet and allowed her to look at it for a moment. "Ma'am," I said softly, gesturing at the clothing in the suitcase, "These were Sarah's things, weren't they? You recognize them. I can see that you do."

Vanessa said nothing, but her expression softened, and she seemed to grow smaller and fold in upon herself as she looked at and then touched some of Sarah's clothing. She lifted out a little white undershirt and held it in her lap, then raised it to her cheek and felt the fabric on her skin. Her lips parted slightly and then trembled. Her eyes became moist and she closed them against the tears.

I sat there and watched Vanessa and tried to imagine the anguish she was feeling all over again at the onslaught of memory triggered by the items in her daughter's suitcase. I hated the idea that I was bringing this dear woman back to the pain that likely caused her to flee from her memories in the first place, and I dreaded what I had to do next.

"Ma'am, you told me you have a husband who is a captain in the army serving in the Philippines."

"Yes," she said, a look of pride coming onto on her face. "My husband is serving with honor and distinction even as we speak."

Now, more than ever, I was sure that at the heart of her delusion was the fervent hope her beloved husband would one day walk through the door and be reunited with her, and I prayed the news I was about to deliver would be cathartic and not add to her sorrow. "I'd like to show you something," I said, and reached into my pocket.

I took out my wallet and flipped to the little window displaying my driver's license. It had been renewed last year and was set to expire in 1964, three years from now. She looked at it and then met my eyes. Next, I produced my fishing license which was issued in March of this year and displayed in bold type the year 1961. "Ma'am," I said, "it is not 1945. It is May 7, 1961. The war in the Philippines ended sixteen years ago."

A look of confusion wrinkled her brow as she looked at the date printed on my fishing license. "Is this some kind of gag, Mr. Ryan?"

"No, ma'am," I said. "The world is no longer at war. Your husband's service to his country came to an end sixteen years ago."

"That is absurd! I will not sit here and listen to one more word from you. What kind of a person would come here and spew such calumny? And to what end? Are you some huckster intent on defrauding me? Is it your habit to trick people with—"

Her words faltered, and her lovely brown eyes became pools. She lowered her face, and a series of sobs shook her shoulders. When again she looked at me, the pain in her eyes was so profound I could hardly bear to return her gaze.

How was I going to do what I had to do next? How was I going to challenge her with evidence that would prove the husband she believed would one day come home had been killed in action? If she believed me at all, this tragic news would likely bring her long season of hopeful waiting to an end, and what was the point? Would she be better off facing reality if it meant abandoning hope and facing anew the very grief that likely had driven her to her present state of mind? Who was I to lay all of this upon her again? I'm not a trained professional, and the truth was that I was fooling with things I knew nothing about. *You could do more harm than good here, Tommy, old boy*, I thought.

All of this ran through my mind, and then I reminded myself that this was about helping Sarah. For some reason, whether metaphysical or spiritual I cannot say, Sarah was bound to the place where she died and not able to move on. If Abe's grandmother was right, a dark presence desired to take Sarah's soul into an empty realm and revel in her despair, which I believed related directly to a severed connection between her and her mother that has persisted since the day Sarah died. I needed Vanessa to remember her little girl and to reach out to her, and her vigil for a man who was never coming home was keeping that from happening.

I stood and opened the suitcase in which I had stowed the envelope containing the documents from the army and the other items I had brought with me. I took out the envelope and sat back down. "Mrs. Reissman," I said, "I have something more to show you." I removed the Western Union Telegram from the envelope and gave it to her. "You've seen this telegram before," I said. "It came to you sixteen years ago, and I am quite sure you read it and learned that your husband had been declared missing in action."

I watched her eyes travel over the page, and as she read it, her hands again began to tremble. "Mrs. Reissman…Vanessa," I said softly, "you did read this telegram when it arrived, didn't you?" She didn't reply, and I said, "I can't imagine how painful that news had to be for you, and I'm sure that on that very day you began praying for news to come that Robert had been located and was safe." I watched for her reaction and then asked softly, "But news didn't come, did it?"

Vanessa remained silent and allowed the telegram to slip from her fingers and fall to the floor. She looked up at me, and the expression in her eyes was so sorrowful that I felt my own begin to well with tears. "You and Sarah began waiting together," I said, "and your waiting went on for three long years."

Again, Vanessa said nothing, so I picked up the envelope with the letter from the War Department, slipped it out, and handed it to her. She took it, and again I watched her eyes scan left to right as she read the words printed there. "Vanessa," I said, "that letter is from the War Department. It's dated June 25, 1948 and the envelope it came in is dated June 29, 1948. You received that letter, and after three long years of waiting for good news, the absolute worst news had arrived. I can't even begin to imagine how you felt, and I am so sorry for your loss."

Vanessa's reaction completely surprised me. I was expecting anger, harsh words, and more denial, but she calmly folded the letter and bent over and picked up the telegram she had dropped on the floor. She sat up and straightened her back and folded her hands in her lap on top of the two documents. She met my eyes and seemed to steel herself.

"My husband is dead, isn't he, Mr. Ryan?" she said.

"Yes, ma'am," I whispered, and found that I could barely speak, so moved was I by the courage I saw in her eyes; something I had not expected to see there.

She said, "I feel as if you have more to share with me, don't you, Mr. Ryan?"

"Yes, ma'am,"

I stood again and opened the suitcase and removed the newspaper Edna Rollins had given to me. I had no intention of showing her the article with its graphic description of the accident. The first paragraph was enough to remind her of what had happened on the day she had received the news from the War Department. I read it to her and waited for her response. When none was forthcoming, I said, "Mrs. Reissman, do you remember packing suitcases that day and preparing to leave Summer Rest?"

Vanessa just stared at me with a confused look in her eyes, so I stood once again and retrieved the Raggedy Ann doll and the locket from the suitcase. I sat back down and reached out to her with the doll. She took it and looked at it for a long moment, and I was sure I could see recognition in her eyes. "That was Sarah's doll, wasn't it?" I asked.

Vanessa opened her mouth to speak but was overcome with emotion; she closed it again and remained silent. I held out the locket and said, "I am sure this belongs to you." She took it gingerly in her fingers, as if it were something sacred. She opened it, and her hand went to her heart at the sight of Sarah's hair coiled on top of the photo. She picked them up and held them to capture the light, and in her eyes, I saw profound grief, weighty, unendurable, and complete. Her eyes moved to the tiny oval-shaped photo of herself with Robert and her five-year-old daughter.

"Oh, my dear lord," she said, and seemed to fold in upon herself. "Robert, Sarah," she moaned, and then Vanessa buried her face in her hands and wept bitterly.

I got up from where I was sitting and sat next to her on the loveseat. I took the locket and strands of hair from Vanessa's hands and set them on a side table and then took her in my arms and held her as she released years of repressed emotion. Her slight frame shook under the immense weight of the sorrow she felt for a family lost to her; a husband and a young daughter not properly mourned.

Chapter 17

I sat beside Vanessa as she sobbed into her hands, struggling to process everything I had told and shown her. Her pain was palpable and quite honestly, more than I could bear. I closed my eyes and prayed that in my bid to help Sarah I had done the right thing in forcing Vanessa to confront the deaths of her husband and daughter. If not, I had no idea what I would do next.

Something landed lightly on my bare arm, and I opened my eyes expecting to see an insect, but that was not at all what I saw. In the brief moment that I had sat with my eyes closed, everything had changed. Where there had been order and neatness, there was now neglect and disuse. It was as if the house had somehow aged and grown dilapidated in mere seconds. It was either that or I had been transported many years into the future. Either way, it made no sense at all, and for a moment, I wondered if I was having some kind of mental episode myself.

The ceiling of the porch had been expertly painted a light gray that contrasted beautifully with the burgundy and cream-colored accents around the doors and windows, but now it was no longer the pristine paint job it had been when I first admired the old Victorian house just yesterday. It looked as if it had not been freshened with a new coat of paint in many years. Large areas were weather-blistered and peeling or faded and chalky. The paint on the railings and great columns on either side of the wide front steps were also flaking. I glanced down at the floor and saw that its dark green paint was no longer flawless. It was now scuffed and faded, and several of the floorboards were black along their edges with water stains and rot.

Everywhere, drifts of dried leaves cluttered the floor of the porch and lay in heaps against the walls and in the corners. A thick layer of dust coated the window glass and rested upon the sills. Gauzy spider webs and a tapestry of old insect cocoons upholstered the corners where the walls of the house and the ceiling of the porch met, and even more stretched between the railings and ornate spindles.

Something was terribly wrong. *I'm losing my mind*, I thought. Nothing looked the same as it did only moments ago. *What in the world is going on?*

I looked at the wicker sofa I was sitting upon and saw that the once colorful and comfortable cushions were split, dry-rotted, dusty, and reeking of mildew. The chair I had been sitting in across from Vanessa was a nest of exploded stuffing. The glass top of the end table next to the chair was shattered and lying in shards on the floor.

I placed my hands on Vanessa's shoulders and pushed her back to look at her face. Her eyes were open but unseeing and expressionless. She was utterly rigid as if gripped with rigor. "Vanessa," I said, and shook her gently. She didn't respond, and I feared that shock had overcome her. I tried several more times to elicit a response, a blink, a tear, a scream, anything, but it was all to no avail. I chastised myself, *Stupid, foolish man. You're no psychologist. What have you done to this poor woman? It was too much. Too much! You better get help!*

I didn't have time to waste trying to figure out what was happening. I stood and moved across the littered porch to the front door, intent on telephoning for help. When I pulled the screen door open, it sagged free of the top hinge and, with a piercing screech that set my teeth on edge, scraped a deep groove in the faded green paint of the porch floor. I stood there, dumbfounded, wondering whether I had come under a delusion of my own.

Get ahold of yourself, Tommy. Get help first; ponder later.

I pushed into the house hoping to find a telephone, though whom I would call and what I would say were beyond me. The front door swung in on stiff hinges, and I stepped into a large formal entry. To my left was a closet; to my right, an ornately carved mahogany console table stood below an enormous dusty mirror. A tall crystal vase sat in the center of the table bristling with the stems of long-forgotten roses whose desiccated petals lay scattered upon the table's dusty surface. I remembered what Vanessa had said to me only yesterday: *"Yellow spring flowers symbolize life, Mr. Ryan. I have cut these to remind me of all those who have lost their lives fighting in this god-awful war."*

I hadn't thought of it at the time, but early May was entirely too early for roses this far north, yet she had handed me a beautiful specimen. It was still lying on the front seat of my truck. I left that to ponder later as well. I had to find a telephone. *Keep first things first, ole sock, ole boy. Keep first things first.*

Directly ahead of me were tall double doors made of solid oak. I pushed through them and entered a large, high-ceilinged hall. A magnificent open staircase lay before me, ascending to a darkened second floor. "Hello," I called out and then listened for a response. I heard nothing and tried again with the same result.

I glanced to my left into what appeared to be a formal dining room. The room was dark, but there was enough light coming through the entry door at my back to make out the shape of a long table arranged with several chairs and what appeared to be a large china hutch against the far wall.

To my right, through a high archway, I could see what appeared to be a darkened living room. I went that way hoping to find a telephone, but when I entered the room, I could see little. Windows hung with heavy draperies blocked daylight as effectively as blackout curtains. Considering the timeframe in which Vanessa believed she was living, it is very likely that is what they were. I found a wall switch and flicked it up and down several times but turned on no lights.

I made my way across the floor to a tall window that rose nearly to the ceiling and pulled back the drapes. Filtered light fell in through dingy glass revealing a room that looked as if it had not been occupied nor cleaned for years. A thick layer of dust covered every surface like velour, and cobwebs festooned every corner. Dead insects lay on the floor by the hundreds. It was like walking through gravel. I drew back a drape on another window to allow more light into the room and then stood still listening for any sound that would indicate somebody else may be in the house. I heard only the sound of my breathing.

I found a telephone on a side table next to a high-backed wing chair and lifted the receiver to listen for a dial tone but hcard nothing. I clicked the cradle several times with no result. The telephone was as dead as the light switches.

I made a quick search of the rest of the ground floor rooms, opening draperies as I advanced through each, but found nothing but the detritus of disuse: dust webs, dead insects, and mice scurrying for cover. The house was utterly abandoned and looked to have been so for years.

I decided to return to Vanessa. I would put her in my truck and drive her into town where I hoped I could find some help for her. There was a clinic. I could start there. I hustled my way back to the grand hall and the front doors, which I had left standing open, and stopped dead in my tracks. Dozens of crows, maybe a hundred or more, covered the floor of the front hall and the bottom-most steps of the staircase. Hundreds of tiny oil-spot eyes cast their gaze in my direction as I slid to a halt. Seeing them inside the house that way gave a whole new definition to the word "unnatural." Crows are harmless birds, but seeing them grouped that way was strangely eerie in a way I will never be able to describe adequately.

I looked through the open entry door and saw dozens more swarming the porch and railings. Just like the crows I had seen sitting high in the big pine tree where I met Sarah and in the salvage yard where I had encountered Robert Reissman, these birds, too, were utterly silent as they hopped here and there vying for space. As I stood inside the grand hall, looking out through the entryway, several more winged in and landed on the porch railing, causing those who had already alighted to shift and make room.

I was going to have to move forward slowly and part the birds by placing each foot carefully in the small gaps between them. I had no desire to crush one and feel the snap of their hollow bones beneath my shoe. A small patch of floor opened up, and I carefully place a foot there. It was a stretch, and I had to put my arms out at my sides for balance. I felt like a tightrope walker at the circus. I was just about to lift my back foot when I felt a sharp pain in my ankle. One of the crows had struck out with its thick beak and jabbed me. It was like a hot needle. I looked, and I saw a small drop of blood bloom on my white sock. Looking down at my ankle caused me to lose my balance, and I began teetering from side to side. I tried to regain my balance by alternately raising and lowering my arms, but it made no difference. I was going to fall and crush several of the crows in the process.

I felt myself moving closer to the tipping point and squatted to lower my center of gravity. Just then, a particularly large crow flew in through the open door and hit me squarely in the chest. I went down hard and heard and felt the sickening crunch of tiny hollow bones snapping. It was like falling on eggshells, and the sound made me want to vomit. Many of the birds took to the air to avoid getting crushed, and for a moment, I was inside a tornado of wings, beaks, and feathers. The air swirled around me and quills slapped my face and raked across my eyes. I had landed squarely on my back and felt several of the crows flatten under my weight. Still-living birds squirmed beneath me. It was like lying on a mattress of golf balls.

The crows were no longer silent. Their cawing was deafening. Their excitement rallied the birds perched on the floor of the porch and on the railing. They began streaming in through the front door, and in an instant, the grand hall was insane with motion. The air was stirred into a frenzy of flapping wings and screaming crows. I tried sitting up, if for no other reason than so I would no longer feel the wounded birds struggling beneath my back, but I could do little more than cover my head and hope they would flee back through the open door.

I remained that way until I could stand it no longer. I had to get up and out of the house. I rolled onto my stomach and steamrolled several more crows in the process. I placed my hands on the floor to push myself up and felt something sticky under my palms. Through it all, I kept my eyes closed to avoid taking a direct hit with a beak to my eye, but my hands told me all I needed to know. Everywhere I placed them, I felt dead or wounded birds. Some pecked violently at my fingers; others landed on my back or tangled themselves in my hair. I felt a beak inserted into my left ear, and I slapped at it madly. I felt a sharp pain above my left eyebrow and, a moment later, blood trickling down my forehead. I could take no more. I screamed with rage and fear and thrust upright, feeling more bones snap and the ugly, liquid sensation of innards beneath my palms.

I managed to rise and began swinging my arms wildly like a man who has fallen into a beehive. Crows slammed into me, hitting my chest, back, and legs. I batted several away as I dashed into the dining room and ducked into a corner as far away from the swarm as I could get. From my vantage point, I could see dozens of dead and dying crows, some lying in pools of blood, some dragging broken wings, others flipped and flopped, unable to stand. Above it all, a massive swarm of crows circled as if caught in a whirlpool, constricting upon itself with every revolution, forming a vertical column like the tail of a funnel cloud.

I stole a glance at myself. My shirt was covered with blotches of blood. Feathers were stuck to my palms and woven into my hair. I had fine down in my mouth, and I spat to rid myself of it. I had been pecked several times, but the wounds were superficial. My real problem was getting past the swirling mass of angry crows and out the front door to Vanessa. I had no desire to dash through that hellacious vortex and crush even more of the frenzied birds. If I were to slip and go down again, it would be more than I could bear, so I stayed put and brushed the feathers from my hair and wiped my palms on my jeans and tried to figure out how best to get outside.

I was just about to use a chair to break a window when I looked into the hall beyond the dining room door. The swirling pillar of crows had changed. Its shape was no longer strictly columnar. The twisting motion slowed, and the column was compressing. I could hardly believe what I was seeing, but its form was becoming vaguely humanoid. I could see a rudimentary head resting upon a broad set of shoulders, and below the shoulders, the shape of a trunk and thick legs and heavy arms. It was tall, maybe nine feet, and growing thicker by the minute as more crows flew in from outside the house to join with it. With the addition of every bird, the ugly thing took on a more defined shape. What had been nothing more than an odd vortex of flying crows was gathering itself into a living nightmare. Bird after bird entered the grand hall and landed on the obscene thing, struggling and forcing themselves into and beneath the surface of its glossy, black skin, disappearing within as if sinking into a pool of tar.

LEAVE HER ALONE!

It was a thick, raspy voice and it reverberated within my skull like the sound of a jackhammer.

YOU WILL NOT TAKE HER FROM THE EMPTY!

I clapped my hands over my ears, but the voice surged into my brain like stormwater through a culvert. I could do nothing to shut off the flow. I felt my breath catch in my lungs, and a wave of dizziness came over me. My knees gave out, and I slid down the wall and landed splay-legged on the floor.

SHE MUST GO INTO THE EMPTY!

I looked up. The profane thing was shambling toward me with a lurching, graceless gait. It shuffled through a drift of dead crows, crunching their tiny bones, flattening them, and trailing blood and offal. Not all of the birds melded entirely with the monster. I saw heads of crows sticking out like warts. Their beaks clicked opened and closed as if gasping for air. Individual wings protruded from the monster's hide, flapping as if trying the give the horrid thing flight. A thousand tiny oil spot eyes blinked at me as the creature drew closer and closer.

SHE MUST GO INTO THE EMPTY!

I had to stand and meet it head-on and put up some form of defense. I pushed back with my legs, scrabbling like a crab, trying to get up, but it was useless. I couldn't get to my feet. The crow-thing—The Empty—that's what it was; the embodiment of the desolate void that stole lost and despairing souls—halved the distance between us; shuffling stiff-legged across the hardwood floor, stepping on the dead and wounded birds that lay in its path, its myriad oil-spot eyes blinking at me. They glared at me with a hatred I could feel in my nerve endings. Its purpose was clear. The Empty intended to claim Sarah for its own, and I was standing in its way.

I am not entirely sure what happened next. My mind was screaming, *GET UP! RUN! YOU HAVE TO MOVE,* but my body refused the order. The Empty stood over me, its myriad black bead eyes blinking and flitting back and forth, staring at me; looking me over, staring into me. Numbness began to creep up my limbs, and I felt myself getting thin. There is no other way to describe it. It was like adding too much water to concentrate. I was a thin, weak, and ineffectual version of my former self.

I shifted my eyes and down. A semi-transparent image of my legs floated above them like a double exposure on camera film. I looked at my hands, a weak copy as thin as mist lifted from my skin. The strange effect spread to the rest of my body, and a moment later, an insubstantial version of me was floating in the air, drifting toward the Empty. All I could do was to sit impotently against the wall. I felt nothing; no floor beneath me, no wall at my back, no draft upon my skin. I was loose. I felt untethered and adrift.

I raised my eyes and could no longer see the room in which I was sitting. I could see only the infinite black beyond creation. I saw the place of utter desolation, and within this unfathomable void, I would know no hope. I would know no love. I would know nothing of time nor distance. It was an endless nothing in which I would forever remember and ceaselessly mourn all that I had been and had lost. I looked into the EMPTY, and I was undone.

I do not know when I realized it, but at some point, I was aware again, and I was shielding my eyes from a blinding white radiance emanating from the area behind the crow-thing. I lifted my hands to shield my eyes and squinted into the light. The creature's outlines were blurred and indistinct, and I got a whiff of something that smelled like burning hair. Smoke began rising from its black, feathery skin. The crow-thing jerked in a violent spasm and started thrashing about, jittering as if performing some horrible parody of a dance. Flames erupted from the center of its chest and filled the entire room with the sickly stench of burning feathers. Within seconds, the thing that would have certainly either killed me or driven me mad was a stinking torch. It spun around a few times, crashing into walls and careening off of the table, flailing its arms. A moment later, it hit the floor with a billow of sparks. Within seconds, it was completely engulfed in flames. Amazingly, the fire ignored the floor and the walls. It was as if it were meant only for the Empty.

With the creature no longer standing before me, I had an unobstructed view of the source of the light. It radiated from the dining room doorway, glowing like a miniature sun. I shielded my eyes and looked at it past my raised hand. A vague feminine shape stood very erect at the center of the glow.

After a moment, I tried and was able to push myself up and stand, though I needed to use the wall for support. I looked again at the glowing figure in the doorway to find it receding into the hall outside the dining room. Upon reaching the center of the hall, the radiance paused for a moment and then moved quickly toward the open door that led outside to the porch. I tried my legs and found them working again, though I had to move slowly. Holding onto the wall for support, I shuffled out of the dining room into the hall and looked outside through the open door. Whatever had come to my rescue had utterly vanished.

Chapter 18

I rested a moment and recovered a bit more, then made my way outside to look for Vanessa. She was no longer sitting on the wicker sofa beneath the large window. I looked across the lawn in the direction of the lake. The once tidy landscape between the house and the shoreline was no longer neat and orderly. The lawn was overgrown and littered with years of fallen leaves. Weeds choked the flowerbeds. Woody underbrush and saplings had sprung up where they hadn't been only an hour ago. The fountain, which had been flowing with clear, clean water tumbling from its multi-level bowels into the reflecting pool, now held stagnant rainwater and rotting leaves. Its once gleaming white finish was stained green with algae. Beyond the fountain, the process of succession was taking over the shoreline of the lake returning it to its natural condition. Where only a short while ago there had been a formal lawn, now a dense thicket of young fir, maple, and birch had sprouted. None of this made any sense at all, but after what had just taken place inside the house, I told myself not to waste any time trying to figure it out.

I called for Vanessa and received no answer. I hobbled down the steps and moved as quickly as my jittery legs would allow and searched the grounds but found no sign of her. I went back into the house and quickly conducted a search but saw only dusty floors and unbroken cobwebs. I decided to go back to my truck and head out to the highway. Perhaps she had decided to walk out to the road and try to catch a ride. I hoped not, but it was the only thing I could imagine she had done. She was indeed nowhere to be found at Summer Rest.

Upon reaching the highway, I looked in both directions. I had no idea how much of a head start she had on me and in which direction she may have walked. One thing was clear, she was nowhere in sight. I decided to drive a distance in both directions, but eventually, I concluded that I wasn't going to find her. If she had walked out to the highway, she likely caught a ride with a passing motorist. I hoped she was alright and that I would have the opportunity to see her again. I had serious concerns about what I did to her in forcing her to face her delusion and the reality of her husband and daughter's death. I wasn't at all sure that I had done the right thing.

The short ride home was a jumble of questions and confusion, and I wondered if I would ever understand what had just happened. I had no idea at all how to rationalize the events of the day. It was clear to me that something dark and brooding had desired to claim Sarah for its own, and I hoped with all my heart that whatever had come to my rescue had destroyed that darkness for good and had not just sent it packing.

I didn't know what to think about Vanessa Reissman and Summer Rest. I was navigating new waters when it came to the supernatural, the metaphysical, and the human psyche. Could Vanessa's delusion have been so powerful she was able to cause me to see Summer Rest the way it had been years ago when it was a happier place to her? There was much I didn't know about Vanessa and the injuries she suffered in the accident. I have heard that humans use only about ten percent of their brains and that amazing possibilities reside within the other ninety percent. I supposed it is possible her head injuries may have activated an ability to project her thoughts into the minds of others. Perhaps Summer Rest itself had conspired with Vanessa to keep up appearances, allowing me to see what it wanted me to see. Either way, I was not likely to get much sleep tonight thinking about it.

Chapter 19

As I approached my driveway, I noticed Doctor Rayburn's truck parked near the garage. A second vehicle, one I didn't recognize, was parked behind it. I turned in and parked next to Doctor Rayburn's truck and saw that he and Dennis Cain were sitting in my lawn chairs in the cool of the shade. I climbed out of my truck and walked over.

"Hello, doctor," I said, "Mr. Cain."

They both stood, and Doctor Rayburn said, "I stopped by to check on the fawn and found Mr. Cain knocking on your door. We decided to wait for a spell and see if you'd show up. I was going to ask you what you decided to do with the fawn and Mr. Cain has some information he wanted to give to you."

I saw them both looking me over, taking notice of my bloodstained shirt and disheveled hair, but neither man asked me about them. Doctor Rayburn stepped past me and said, "I'll check in on the little guy and let the two of you talk."

We took a seat and watched Doctor Rayburn walk across my yard and slip into the garage. Dennis said, "I did some checking after you left, used my reporter's know-how and contacts to poke under a few rocks and see what slithered out. I learned a few things I thought you might be interested to know."

"What's that," I said, thinking about all I could tell him if I ever decided to tell anyone about my experiences of the last hour. But it was unlikely I would tell anyone what had happened to me at Summer Rest. Sometimes, when the truth is unbelievable, the better part of wisdom is to keep it to yourself.

Dennis said, "I made a few calls to a friend of mine who is on staff with the *Chicago Tribune* and asked him to see what he could find out about whatever happened to Vanessa Reissman. I gave him the name of her aunt, Sarah Goldman, provided him with the relevant dates and enough detail to do some digging, and left him to it. He called me back this morning."

I had been listening while looking into the shadows under the firs at the edge of my yard, hoping to see the doe lurking there, but now looked directly at Mr. Cain.

"My friend called me back with an obituary for Sarah Goldman," Dennis said. He took a notebook from his shirt pocket and flipped past several pages before finding the one he wanted. "As it turns out, she died peacefully in her sleep about eight years ago at the ripe old age of ninety-two. The obit listed her kin, both dead and alive, and in doing so, revealed the following: Sarah, Mrs. Hirsh Goldman, was preceded in death by several relatives, actually," he said with a grin, "virtually all of them slipped beyond the veil before dear Aunt Sarah gave up the ghost. Among those was one Vanessa, Mrs. Robert Reissman, who in August of 1948 succumbed to injuries sustained in an automobile accident while vacationing at the family retreat in Northern

Wisconsin. Tragically, the accident also took the life of her eight-year-old daughter, Sarah Marie."

I couldn't speak. I just sat there with what I am sure was a stupefied expression on my face. Vanessa Reissman, the woman who had spoken with me on her lawn, who had offered me shade and ice water on her porch, who had given me a yellow rose, and who had sat next to me crying on my shoulder only a short while ago, had died within a few months of returning to Chicago to recover from the injuries she had suffered in the accident. All my encounters with Vanessa, like those with her daughter, had been with her spirit.

I was dumbstruck. Was there nothing connected with Summer Rest that I could take at face value? Was anything that happened to me over the past few days anything more than some grand illusion? Vanessa was so real, our interactions so earthly and physical, that it never even crossed my mind that I had been interacting with anything other than a grieving woman immersed in personal tragedy.

"Tommy."

It did go a long way toward answering many of the questions I had running through my mind. Just like Sarah, Vanessa, too, had looked, sounded, and felt utterly corporeal. I had touched her, and she had touched me. She had handed me a glass of water and a flower she had presumably cut from her garden. It had never occurred to me that she was anything other than a living woman.

"Tommy."

With Sarah, I had seen first-hand her power to project images and to interact with the physical realm. Vanessa also had this ability, and she used it masterfully to make Summer

Rest appear as grand and well-maintained as it had been when the Reissman family lived there during happier times. I suppose I saw the estate the way she wanted it to be and not the way it was now. Only after I confronted Vanessa with the deaths of her husband and her daughter did her spirit stop projecting and allow me to see things as they really are.

"Tommy."

I shook my head to clear away my thoughts and said, "Yes."

"You seemed to have gone wool-gathering for a minute," Dennis said. "I was saying, after burying little Sarah, Aunt Sarah transferred Vanessa to a private medical facility in Chicago to recover from her injuries which, apparently, she did not do."

Dennis Cain closed his notebook. I went back to staring at the forest and doing my best to keep from pondering the remarkable things I had experienced over the past few days until later when I was alone and free to think.

"I appreciate you coming out here to tell me that," I said. "It answers a lot of questions for me but raises even more, like, who now owns Summer Rest?"

"I can tell you that," he said, and opened his notebook again. "I was curious about that too, so I checked with the Registrar of Deeds at the courthouse. The home is now the property of a distant relation, one Stella Ableman. Ms. Ableman resides in Warsaw Poland. She pays the property taxes promptly every year but is rumored to have never set foot upon the estate."

I thought about that for a moment as I recalled seeing the light come on outside of Summer Rest when Sarah pointed it out to me across the lake. It must have been a dusk-to-dawn light that comes on automatically in the evening to provide a modicum of security for the unoccupied home.

Dennis got up from his chair, and I stood as well. We shook hands, and he said, "It looks like that accident was more tragic than we knew. Life interrupted," he said. I walked him over to his car and watched him back down my driveway. Doctor Rayburn came up beside me. He was carrying the fawn.

"Here's your chance," he said, and pointed at the woods where the doe was standing just far enough back in the shade to feel hidden from us. I felt my heart race as I realized the moment of truth had come. Would there be a reunion or a rejection? Would the mother welcome her little one and resume caring for him, or would that task fall to me? I was about to find out.

Doctor Rayburn reached toward me with the fawn, and I slipped my arms under his chest and beneath his haunches and felt his silky fur against my forearms. He made no fuss at all, having adjusted quickly to human interaction. That worried me. He would be better off fearing humans, but I supposed that if he were reunited with his mother, he would soon forget his time with me and the care Doctor Rayburn and I had provided. That would be best for all.

I walked slowly toward the edge of my lawn, keeping my eyes on the doe, looking for any reaction, any flinch or twitch of the big muscles in her haunches that would signal she was about to bolt. To my surprise, she remained where she stood, even as I approached to within ten yards of her hiding place. I was sure she could hear my heart pounding in my chest. I know I could.

I stopped about twenty paces from the tree line and bent over and gingerly set the fawn down in the open where the doe could see him clearly, then backed away, keeping my eyes on both animals. I made it all the way back to where I had left Doctor Rayburn, and then the two of us slipped around the corner of my cabin to watch from a place of concealment.

At first, I thought I had failed. The fawn just stood there in the open, statue-like, not moving a muscle, but then the doe emerged slowly from the woods, sunlight luminous on her summer-red fur, and walked stiffly to the fawn. He saw her approaching, and his tiny flag of a tail started pin-wheeling, as it was prone to do at feeding times. He gave a little sideways hop, kicking his hind legs out wildly behind him and started toward her. They met nose to nose, and then the doe sniffed at the plaster and gauze wrap on her baby's leg. She looked toward my cabin, as if making the connection, and then turned toward the woods and began walking. The fawn immediately set about trying to nurse, even as he walked clumsily beneath his mother who would likely be happy for the relief a nursing baby would bring to her. A moment later, they were gone.

Doctor Rayburn congratulated me on a job well done, and I thanked him for all his help. He said something about heading into town to do some reading at the library, and I walked him to his truck and watched him drive away. I spent the rest of the evening straightening out the garage and changing the oil on my old truck. Later, after a supper of hamburger steak and fried potatoes, I took a cup of coffee out to the lawn chairs to watch darkness rise out of the fir trees to pool in the evening sky and to think. I didn't see any deer at all.

Chapter 20

Sunday dawned clear and breezy. After breakfast, I made the drive into town and attended services at the little community church where I used to sit with my mother and father every week without fail, right up until the time my father became too sick to attend church. I am sure the pastor preached a rousing sermon, but I must confess, I had trouble paying attention and couldn't tell you what he preached about, but afterward, most of the congregation went forward at the altar call and stayed long after service ended. I like a good altar call as much as the next guy, but I made my way out to my truck instead and headed for Summer Rest. I needed to look at it again, to see what face it was presenting today, and to secure the front door.

Things made a bit more sense now that I understood why the driveway had been so overgrown. Vanessa's power to project an image of a happier, more contented Summer Rest hadn't extended far enough to include the driveway. I parked in my usual place and walked onto the property. The house and grounds of the grand estate looked the same as when I had left it yesterday—overgrown, disused, and falling into disrepair. The place just looked, if you will ,

167

pardon the pun, dispirited. I wondered if that was an indication that Vanessa's spirit was no longer in residence.

I made my way onto the front porch and caught a glimpse of something lying on the floor by the wicker furniture. I walked over and picked it up. It was the envelope containing the Western Union Telegram and the letter from the War Department I had shown to Vanessa the day before. I took it with me and walked to the open front door where I hesitated before going inside. I had no desire to encounter the horrible thing that had tried to take me into that god-awful void, and I listened and looked carefully before stepping inside. When I finally entered the vestibule, I placed the envelope on the table next to the vase with the dead roses.

After several more seconds of listening, I stepped into the great hall and looked at the wide staircase rising to the levels above me and decided not to venture up there. I looked around. Numerous tiny mounds of dust were scattered about on the floor. I squatted and scooped up a small amount of the powder and sifted it through my fingers. It was quite fine and coal-black in color. I took a sniff and detected the odor of burnt feathers. I could see more of the piles inside the dining room, and I walked in there. Near the end wall, where I had collapsed yesterday, incapacitated by the crow-thing, was a much larger pile of the silty, black dust. I walked over and nudged it with my boot and thought about the white light that had intervened yesterday. There had been a woman-like form glowing at the center of the radiance. Had that been Vanessa? Had she come to my rescue by manifesting some sort of spectral power reducing the terrible crow-thing and its complement of crow minions to piles of fine carbon? I think that is precisely what happened.

I turned and retraced my steps until I was standing again on the big porch. I closed the front door but had no key to lock it. I then made a trip around the entire house making sure all the windows were intact. Summer Rest wasn't my responsibility, but I had no idea how long it would be before anybody would come to check on the old house, and to make sure it was still weathertight was the least I could do for Vanessa and Robert Reissman.

I left Summer Rest and started for home, and as I approached the place where I had first seen Sarah, the place where she had died thirteen years ago, I slowed and pulled over onto the gravel shoulder of the road. Warmth came into my eyes and my vision blurred with tears. Seated on the log near the big pine tree were Sarah and Vanessa. Both were in their Sunday best, Sarah in her bright, yellow sundress and wide-brimmed hat, Vanessa in a lovely pink, ankle-length dress and black pillbox hat trimmed with baby roses.

I fished a handkerchief from my back pocket and wiped my eyes. I rolled down my window for a better view and watched as mother and daughter stood together holding hands. They smiled warmly at me, and then little Sarah raised her tiny gloved hand to her lips and blew me a kiss. I pretended to catch it and then placed my hand over my heart where that kiss would reside for the rest of my life.

I didn't get out of my truck, and they didn't approach me. I just sat there for a long moment smiling back at them, and then I raised my hand in farewell and put my old truck in gear. I drove off watching Sarah and Vanessa in my rearview mirror until they faded from view.

I never saw them again or ever went back to Summer Rest, but I did do one last thing. The following Sunday after church, I drove back to the big pine and retrieved the cross Abe Johnson had placed there so long ago. I took it home with me, and in my garage, I sanded it down until it was clean and smooth. I repainted it with several coats of white enamel so it would withstand Wisconsin's ever-changing weather, and then using black paint, carefully repainted SARAH and 1948. In the center of the cross, where the members joined with several wraps of bright new wire, I attached a Star of David I had fashioned from oak lath I bought at the lumberyard in Joshua Falls.

The next day, I drove to Johnson's Auto Salvage and picked up Abe. He was dressed in his best suit, and I found myself smiling at the incongruity of this big man, with his calloused and rough grease-stained hands, working to get the knot of his tie perfectly centered in his collar.

"I think this is mighty nice of you, Tommy," he said. "I should have done this years ago. I want to thank you for giving me the chance to put things right."

There were tears in his eyes, and he self-consciously tugged a handkerchief from his pocket and dabbed them away. I reached across the seat and patted him on the shoulder, then put my truck in gear, and we headed for Eagle Bluff.

When we arrived, I pulled over and put the truck in park. "Are you ready for this?" I asked Abe. He nodded, and we got out. We walked through the deep ditch-grass until we were standing before the big pine tree with the healed-over scar near its base. Abe took two yarmulkes from his hip pocket and handed one to me. We placed the skullcaps on our heads, and then Abe closed his eyes and turned his face toward heaven and began reciting the Yizkor in Hebrew. I thought it a fitting prayer, in that *Yizkor,* the first word in the prayer, means remember. I didn't think I would ever forget Sarah and Vanessa.

Wordlessly, I prayed with Abe as he implored God to remember the souls of Vanessa, Sarah, and Robert, and asked Him to elevate them to their celestial home. And I felt conviction as he finished the prayer by pledging to give to charity, and in so doing, accomplish a positive physical deed performed in a world where the departed could no longer exist. It was a beautiful thought, and I silently pledged to give to others more of my time and my fortune, meager though it was.

The prayer was over, and as we stood together in silence, I somehow felt a strengthened connection between Abe and me and our departed friends, and it gave me a warm feeling that I knew would be with me from now on until the end of my days.

There was only one thing more to do. Abe and I returned to my truck, and I rummaged around in my toolbox and came up with a large screwdriver. We walked over to the edge of the forest, and as Abe held it firmly in place, I used two large wood screws to fasten Sarah's cross with the Star of David at its center to the trunk of the big pine tree about five feet above the ground where no snowplow could touch it.

Later that night, after the supper dishes had been washed and dried and put away, I took a cup of coffee with me and stepped outside to look at the stars. The humidity was low, and the sky was amazingly clear. The stars and planets seemed close enough to pluck from the heavens. I thought about the fawn and wondered if I would ever see him again and whether I would ever feel comfortable hunting the woods around my cabin. I figured I would be alright hunting this fall since the little buck would be too small to be a target, but I suspected that my deer hunting days were coming to an end.

The moon was a thin crescent floating in the eastern sky above the tall firs. I am not a believer in astrology. I have always believed that we make our own luck by our actions and the words we choose to pass around, but I had read that in the realm of astrology, the moon is believed to govern our subconscious and our emotional reactions to new circumstances. It is supposed to influence our relationship with our mother and the way we deal with childhood wounds. I was blessed to have a wonderful mother, and despite my father passing away when I was only ten years old, I look back on my childhood and find good memories there, and it saddens me to think of all the memories never created for Sarah.

Standing below the vast canopy of God's creation, I knew I would often think of little Sarah and her mother. I hoped they were finally reunited as a family with Robert in whatever plain of existence came next. I hoped there was a home like Summer Rest sitting majestically on the shore of a shimmering lake with lace curtains billowing on the breeze. I hoped it was surrounded by a verdant, green forest ringing with the music of nature's glee club. I hoped there were flowers for Vanessa to tend and a green lawn with a gleaming, white fountain. I hoped Sarah was making new memories to stand in for those she didn't make here. I hoped they were all happy and contented.

Being the perpetual optimist that I am, I could do nothing clsc, so I hopcd.

THE END